MY MOTHER
MADAME EDWARDA
THE DEAD MAN

MY MOTHER
MADAME EDWARDA
THE DEAD MAN

Georges BATAILLE

Translated by Austryn Wainhouse
with essays by Yukio Mishima and Ken Hollings

MARION BOYARS
LONDON • NEW YORK

First published in hardcover in Great Britain and the United States in 1989 by
MARION BOYARS PUBLISHERS LTD
24 Lacy Road, London SW15 1NL
Republished in paperback in Great Britain and the United States in 1995

www.marionboyars.co.uk

Distributed in Australia and New Zealand by Peribo Pty Ltd
58 Beaumont Road, Kuring-gai, NSW 2080

Reprinted in 1996, 2000, 2003
10 9 8 7 6 5 4 3

My Mother originally published in French as *Ma Mère* by Jean-Jacques Pauvert in 1966.
© Société Nouvelle des Editions Pauvert, 1966, 1979
Madame Edwarda, first published in this translation by *Evergreen Review*.
Originally published in French as *Madame Edwarda* by Jean-Jacques Pauvert in 1956
© Société Nouvelle des Editions Pauvert, 1956
The Dead Man first published in this translation in *Works* Fall/Winter issue 1969.
Originally published in French as *Le Mort* by Jean-Jacques Pauvert in 1967
© Société Nouvelle des Editions Pauvert, 1967
'Georges Bataille and Divinus Deus' from *Shosetsu Tōha Nanima* by Yukio Mishima.
© Yukio Mishima 1968-1970
'In the Slaughterhouse of Love' first published in *Performance* 1984
© Ken Hollings 1984, 1986, 1995, 2000, 2003
'Autobiographical Note' first published in *October* 36 in 1986 © MIT 1986

© These translations MARION BOYARS PUBLISHERS 1989, 1995, 2000, 2003

A CIP catalogue record for this book is available from the British Library.
A CIP catalog record for this book is available from the Library of Congress.

ISBN 0-7145-3004-2

Typeset in 11/13 Baskerville and Optima by Ann Buchan (Typesetters), Middlesex
Printed in Great Britain by Bookmarque Ltd, Croyden, Surrey

PUBLISHER'S
NOTE

When Jonathan Cape first published Austryn Wainhouse's translation of *My Mother* it was with the
explanation that the manuscript for this novel was found
among Georges Bataille's papers at his death. It was almost
complete and ready for the printer. However, the last pages
were confused, much altered and on numerous occasions
offered several versions of the same passage. Bataille's French
publishers thought it best to reproduce only such parts as
were unmistakably clear, and to provide a resumé of the more
confusing sequences from this part of the manuscript.

Madame Edwarda appeared under the pseudonym Pierre
Angélique in two small underground editions of about 50
copies each in 1941 and 1945. It was finally published under
Bataille's own name by Jean-Jacques Pauvert in 1956.
Bataille's foreword to *Madame Edwarda* was also printed as a
separate essay in his book *Eroticism* which is available from
Marion Boyars.

Together, *Madame Edwarda* and *My Mother* formed part of a
larger work to be entitled *Divinus Deus*. However, this project
was still incomplete at the time of Bataille's death, although

many notes, plans and drafts exist for it, and the title has also appeared in subsequent versions of both *Madame Edwarda* and *My Mother*.

Austryn Wainhouse has supplied a note on the manuscript of *The Dead Man* and its origins which is presented here as part of the preface to the text. In the case of all three texts Austryn Wainhouse has revised his original translations for this edition.

Yukio Mishima's *Georges Bataille and Divinus Deus* in this current volume was taken from a collection of his literary essays entitled *What Is the Novel?* It originally appeared as a book review shortly before his tragic death.

In the Slaughterhouse of Love was first published in Performance Magazine in 1984 and was originally presented as a collaboration between Ken Hollings and the artist, Roberta M. Graham. It was later presented as a taped lecture at the ICA in London as part of an installation by Roberta Graham and Ken Hollings in 1985.

The bringing together of these diverse texts gives us an opportunity to examine for ourselves the startling and original ideas of a French writer and philosopher who has exercised a vital influence on contemporary literature and thought.

Marion Boyars Publishers

CONTENTS

Yukio Mishima

GEORGES BATAILLE AND DIVINUS DEUS

I have recently read two extremely fine novels, and I must write about them here since the vivid after-effect of reading them felt incomparable to that of anything else.

They were called *Madame Edwarda* and *My Mother*, from a book entitled *Divinus Deus* by Georges Bataille. In the past, Japanese readers of Bataille have been afflicted by bad translations. This time, however, the translation by Kosaku Ikuta has clearly come out better.

The writers I pay most attention to in modern Western literature are Georges Bataille, Pierre Klossowski, and Witold Gombrowicz. This is because in their work there can be found a vivid, harsh, shocking and immediate connection between metaphysics and the human flesh that forms a direct link between the 18th and 20th centuries, by-passing the 19th. These works reveal an anti-psychological delineation, anti-realism, erotic intellectualism, straightforward symbolism, and a perception of the universe hidden behind all of these, as well as many other common characteristics.

Bataille's *Madame Edwarda* is a novel that demonstrates the manifestation of God to man, and is at the same time a work that is extreme in its obscenity. The narrator pays for Madame Edwarda, a prostitute who calls herself God, at the whorehouse 'The Mirrors'. He then follows Edwarda when she wanders out, wearing a black domino covering her face

and naked body, witnesses her sudden fit and helps her into a
taxi where he sees a manifestation of the true God in Edwarda
who sits on top of, and copulates with, the taxi driver.

When read together with *My Mother*, it will be noticed that
the image of the mother overlaps with that of Edwarda, and
with it a vision of defilement, of incest which violates the
sanctity of the Sacred Mother. But, in these works, the Sacred
Mother does not suffer passively as a victim of trespass; she
herself spurs others on and forces them into an experience,
filled with terror, repulsion and ecstasy, which leads them to
witness God.

However, my aim here is not to develop a theory on
Bataille. I have too many things that I would like to say about
Bataille in this limited space.

What is certain, nevertheless, is that, being aware that the
sacred quality hidden in the experience of eroticism is
something impossible for language to reach (this is also due to
the impossibility of re-experiencing anything through language), Bataille still expresses it in words. It is the
verbalization of a silence called God, and it is also certain that
a novelist's greatest ambition could not lie anywhere else but
here. A woman was chosen to represent the God, who appears
in the novel through the essential unity of the spirit and the
flesh embodied in woman, and the recognition that the
mother (thought to represent the highest virtue in woman)
and the whore (thought to represent the dirtiest) both originate
from the very same part of that flesh: you may recall the words
of Baudelaire who called God a representative of whores.

It is an impossible task to appreciate Bataille in a
business-like manner with these intellectual interpretations,
but in order to read this novel (especially its translated text!) it
is necessary to suppose that only the part that managed to
break through the limits of language is left.

In the preface, Bataille says: 'If there is nothing that
surpasses our powers and our understanding, if we do not
acknowledge something greater than ourselves, greater than

we are *despite ourselves*, something which at all costs must not be, then we do not reach the *insensate* moment towards which we strive and which at the same time we exert all our power to stave off.'

This 'insensate moment' is, needless to say, the moment in which God, grotesque and fearful, appears.

'. . . the existence in us, during these interludes, exists through nothing but a sustaining and ruinous excess, when the fullness of horror and that of joy coincide . . . What, leaving aside the representation of excess, does truth signify if we do not see that which exceeds sight's possibilities, that which it is unbearable to see as, in ecstacy, it is unbearable to know pleasure?'

A very typical Christian way of thought is apparent in Bataille's idea that, in short, God does not manifest himself while our being remains in its proper, balanced form; and only when our existence exceeds this life and leaves behind it something like the outlines of the people left on the stone steps of Hiroshima after the atomic bomb was dropped, then will God manifest himself. What is unique is his utilization of 'eroticism and pain' in the extreme as a means of attaining it.

Madame Edwarda begins with a simple paragraph introducing the narrator, a very typical, lascivious drunkard. Having witnessed 'two furtive whores sneaking down the stair of a urinal', the narrator, haunted by lust and anguish, starts on a drinking spree from one bar to another as the day goes by. This introduction is over in six lines.

The story takes a sudden turn in the following paragraph. The drunkard, who could not control the urge 'to be laid as bare as was the night', takes his trousers off in the street to 'hold my straight-risen sex'.

What is about to happen? Suddenly the rules of the world fall down with his trousers. With frightful speed, the story takes the narrator to the whorehouse 'The Mirrors' and introduces him to the whore, Madame Edwarda.

Truly French simplicity abounds in the description —

dizzy, as if rushing up a spiral staircase — of taking her from
the crowd consumed by blind drunkenness and sexual
provocation, to her room, and of their copulating. The
woman, having raised one leg, pulls at the skin of her thighs
with both hands and shows off her 'hairy and pink crack, just
as full of life as some loathsome squid', then declares herself to
be GOD. All these descriptions, through their simplicity, speed
and density, are elegant. Elegance, as far as literature is
concerned, is nothing but a question of having a straight
posture. (I recall, with interest, Fumiyo Enji's criticism of
Akiyuki Nosaka's *Erojishitachi*, where she described it simply
with the word 'elegant'.) And in following the whore's ritual of
'the lady going up', Madame Edwarda has risen from amidst
disorder and foulness, with a dignity and splendour which is
almost tragic, and which reminds us of Jean Genet's
technique of glorifying filth. It is undoubtedly a 'royal
consecration'.

Now, this short novel is intended as a horrifyingly simple
testimony to God's existence, and into its structure is
woven a feeling of suspense, as in a thriller: when does God
manifest himself to man and when is God's existence borne
out? It is constructed with great care as if it were a one-act
play. In the first scene — where the narrator meets Madame
Edwarda, sleeps with her, and pursues Edwarda who puts on
a domino cloak over her naked body and suddenly leaves —
the narrator does not yet reach the experience of witnessing
God although Edwarda herself bears the name of God, and
the proof of God's existence is still omitted.

Then, when the narrator sees Edwarda in black, standing
under an arch, 'as distressing as an emptiness, a hole', he,
who, through sexual discharge, has been freed from her and is
thus freed from intoxication, recognizes that Edwarda, as she
herself has declared, is GOD.

It can be argued, however, that this is in fact a theoretical
God, a Cartesian God that was reached through the intellect
awoken from sensual lust, through an illumination. This is, in

a sense, this ingenious novelist's trick. Moreover, in this central scene, the writer lets a woman in black clothes and a mask run around the deserted big city late at night, and creates a mysterious atmosphere, so completely different from the previous scene, as if to invite the reader into a gigantic temple. Here Edwarda suddenly convulses and exposes her white naked body, writhing in a spasm, in front of the narrator and the reader, like a white crack in the darkness.

It is the narrator who is watching: it is the narrator who is spending, with a kind of cold anxiety, the time that shifts little by little, inside the nothingness of seeing, like the sand in an hourglass, the essence of one's own existence towards an object. She calls herself God and the narrator, too, recognizes GOD. It is about this time that God could be seen. When will He appear? Before this despair and anguish, and the spasm in Edwarda's naked white body (which is the physical manifestation of them both), the narrator almost touches the crack between sufficiency of being and excess of being, but never quite . . .

But . . .

'Something leaped in my heavy despair.'

'The fever's desiccating ecstasy was issuing out of my utter inability to check myself.'

'Ecstasy' is again needed!

Hence the narrator falls from a hitherto almost mathematical depiction into one of derangement. Words are cast off and he becomes trapped in a struggle — 'I shall have written in vain'. This comment on the impossible, its inaccessibility through language, is not a mere full stop in the novel, but constitutes a sub-plot towards the erotic experience of witnessing God in the last scene.

The novel reaches its true climax in a taxi in the final scene. The scene of copulation with the taxi driver consists of ten or so lines, in which a glimpse can be caught of the darkest abyss of human existence, at the same time as that of the pure and clear, twilight domain which arises from there. Here Bataille shows a force of impact as a novelist, which momentarily dazzles.

The word 'God' is no longer used explicitly. The narrator attains abandonment, relinquishes even seeing, and confesses 'my own distress and fever seemed small things to me'. But then God in fact manifests himself at that very moment, and it becomes certain that the narrator did see God.

Madame Edwarda is indeed a peculiar novel. Although it can seem an arbitrary, undisciplined work compared to, for instance, an exemplary classic short novel such as Prosper Mérimée's *Matteo Falcone*, there is a hidden strict classical structure within it, if you read it carefully. You come to appreciate that the choking intensity ferments as a result of such a classical composition.

Georges Bataille's *My Mother* is a medium-length work that takes the form, as a complete change from *Madame Edwarda*, of a French-style classic of the psychological novel. In fact this remains a mere form, and from *My Mother* we learn that Bataille is a writer proficient in those classical techniques of ordinary novelists. Although he could easily make do with those techniques only, he, boldly, did not find interest in anything but the very subjects that undermine the deepest roots that those techniques are founded upon. This is how, as a result, he becomes for the reader an author who is extremely fastidious but rewarding.

The narrator was a seventeen year-old youth when his father died. It was 1906. He hated his father — who, in his drunkenness, used to torment his wife — and once even considered entering the Church as a revolt against his anti-clericalism. Finally, however, he gives up the idea of becoming a priest in order to live with his mother: she is to him sacred, and he worships her.

Up until then, in the boy's eyes, his mother has been a sorrowful, innocent victim of the tyrannical father: he, dissipated by drinking, women and gambling; she, a sweet, beautiful being who calls her boy 'my gallant lover'. Up to that point the boy solely desired to be her perfect knight. So far, it is a commonplace story, and the simple beginning consists of several fine paragraphs that, while stripped of rhetoric, are still quite exquisite.

Of the secret drinking habit of the sad, beautiful mother, the boy was aware even when his father was still alive. But with the father's death, the image of the mother is radically transformed. She makes the unexpected confession that she is even worse than the father: 'Her hideous, distraught smile was the smile of woe.'

The boy's whole life, to his surprise, had depended upon plots 'contrived' by parental solicitude. 'Later she was to borrow a phrase from my father. "Just lay the blame for everything on me." That was his wish, understanding that in my eyes mother was beyond reproach and must at all costs remain that way.'

The truth is gradually revealed. At the end his mother commits suicide. Here are her words, that could have been her will: 'What I want is that you love me even unto my death. For my part, it is in death that I love you at this very instant. But I don't want your love unless you know I am repulsive, and love me even as you know it.'

This story which, as a climax to this perversion and madness, concludes in a scene of sacred incest in which spirituality is unveiled, is one that I can only leave to the reader to appreciate. But for me, it would be certain that this work managed to satisfy a thirst that no recent Japanese novel could assuage.

As the truth about the boy's mother is exposed, Bataille's writing leaves the gentle, moderate style that has been maintained so far. And as if to prove that the walls of this comfortable home, which had seemed so stable, were in fact merely made of cardboard, he thrusts out one sharp blade after another and carries on ripping away in an excess of brutality.

'I want to read contempt in your eyes, contempt and fear.'
This was the last wish expressed by the mother, both as a
mother and as a woman. To corrupt someone is to awaken
them to truth, and she must be the personification of that
truth — the truth she adheres to — not its mouthpiece: in
short, she has, ultimately, to be 'God' herself. This is probably
the fundamental structure of Bataille's novels, and I
sometimes detect the remains of an eighteenth century Deism
in Bataille; remains of which lead the mother to say: 'It is only
in debauchery that I feel most lucid.'

What is this sincere love that drives her to let others
(moreover, her beloved son) experience a vision of God? She,
a disciple of Sappho?

For us reading a novel is a half sensual, half intellectual,
investigative experience. The hope and anxiety — 'what is
going to happen?' — and the hope for a solution to questions
of 'why?' 'what for?' 'who?': these are the naive, fundamental
desires of anyone who gives themselves up to reading novels,
whatever their quality. The *Bildungsroman* often uses the first
person, as that voice is the easiest to communicate
sensations to the reader. It is the genre in which the reader
identifies with the hero, and which, by arousing the reader's
intellectual curiosity and his will to know, makes them retrace
in a short period the whole process through which the hero
develops — which, in reality, is stretched over many long
years.

Bataille's novels set their face against such a conception —
they might be called an education in corruption — but the
fundamental structures of the two are very similar. Namely
this is a novel so designed that the narrator represents the
reader's own naive investigative desire, his desire to
intellectually analyze, his self-consciousness, his lyricism, his
sexual desire, etc. Thus the reader, as an inevitable result of
those desires, is forced to face the truth, the truth which he
would otherwise never want to see but could no longer avoid,
and, only by going through this loathing and horror, witnesses
the truth that is God.

Then what is the 'mother'? The mother is a seducer who tempts us towards God, she is even God herself. She is well aware that she is the only path through which one is seduced to the Highest Truth, the path of sensuality; and this path must lead into derangement. Her love is cruel, she does not lose herself but leads the other party astray, leads them to the border of destruction. Whipping them mercilessly, she severely demands of them the last arousal of their desires, be they of the flesh or of the spirit.

'You still do not know what I know.' The words the mother speaks to her son — at his last gasp, entangled in the truth he has just found out about the corruption of his mother — are evidently words of God.

Looked at from one point of view, however, God is an idler, an immovable whore lain on a bed. It is always the human who is forced to labour, forced to make efforts, to be knocked down. No novel attempting to depict God's side can be more than a fragment of subtle despair, into which is mixed love and intellectual frustration in the face of the absurdity of man (the son). God is like a hippopotamus, motionless in tropical mud: 'Your mother is only at peace in the mire.'

Bataille dispassionately points out that men's denial of God, the desperate cry of denying the existence of God, does, in fact, 'not come from their true heart'. That 'true heart' embodies the very core of what we call Bataille's 'eroticism'. After all, was it not thanks to him that this abyss of eroticism was opened up to us, an abyss which a certain vulgar Viennese psychoanalyst was evidently incapable of exploring?

Nevertheless, as I said earlier, Bataille never neglects to weave into this erotic metaphysical novel well-planned 'psychological procedures' that are central to the novel. Indeed it can only be a psychological novelist who can make the mother 'feel no peace in her soul until', having made her innocent son tidy up his dead father's desk so that he would find a collection of pornographic photographs and, having foreseen his disgust, 'she could share that repulsion with her son in order that this shared emotion raise her into a state of madness.'

It is as an immediate consequence that tenderness overflows like honey; like a wave, love rises up with shared suffering and sweet beauty from which a cruelty will arise.

And in order to carefully prepare the novel's denouement, the incestuous act consummated between mother and son, the writer deliberately reveals the outcome — the mother's suicide — and hints that her suicide springs as much from her remorse for the situation where, eventually, she did not have any choice but to invite her son into her bed, as from despair: 'I did not desire my mother, she did not desire me.' This, incidentally, is no more than a psychological analysis, a procedure to convince the reader. That is enough as a psychological delineation for a novel. However, since it was not the writer's intention to represent a mere personal psychological tragedy, he deliberately forewarns the reader so that once he is assured of the ending, Bataille is prepared to push the reader into the spiritual and intellectual incest between mother and son, which is ultimately more horrifying, more sensual and more 'corrupt' than physical incest.

The mother herself says: 'the mind's pleasure, fouler than the body's, is purer and the only one whose edge never dulls. Vice, in my view, is like the mind's dark radiance which blinds and of which I am dying. Corruption is the spiritual cancer reigning in the depths of things.'

What was 'man' to her, a disciple of Sappho?

'A man never occupied her thoughts, never penetrated except to satiate her desert where she burned, where her wish seemed to be that, along with her, the silent beauty of anonymous and undifferentiated persons undergo foul destruction. In this kingdom of lust there was no room for tenderness: the gentle and loving were banned from this place, described in the words of the Evangelist: *Violenti rapiunt Illuid.* My mother destined me to that violence over which she reigned.'

MY MOTHER

This final confession in the novel *My Mother* is a horrifyingly tense soliloquy; I will not, however, quote it here as its true depth only speaks to the emotion of someone who has read the whole book.

Translated by Ken Hollings
and Akiko Hada

Terror unendingly renews with advancing age. Without end, it returns us to the beginning. The beginning that I glimpse on the edge of the grave is the *pig* in me which neither death nor insult can kill. Terror on the edge of the grave is divine and I sink into the terror whose child I am.

'Pierre!'

It was a low voice, soft and insistent. Had someone in the next room called me? Called me quietly, so as not to wake me if I were asleep? But I was awake. Had I wakened the way I used to do as a child when I was ill and my mother called to me in that apprehensive voice?

Now it was I who called. But there was no one there, nor was there anyone in the next room.

After a while I realized that in my sleep, dreaming, I had heard my name spoken and that the feeling it left me with was to remain beyond my grasp.

I was deep down in bed, feeling neither disagreeable nor pleasant. All I knew was that during the illnesses and long fevers of my childhood that voice had called to me in the same way; at those times when a mortal danger hanging over me gave my mother, when she spoke, that extreme gentleness.

I was in a sober, attentive frame of mind, and found it odd not to be unwell. This time the burningly intimate memory of my mother did not hurt me. It was no longer mingled with the horror of the smutty laughter I had often overheard.

My father died in 1906 when I was seventeen.

As I was often sick, I had spent a considerable period in a village, living with my grandmother, where my mother would sometimes come and stay. But by that time I had been living in Paris for three years. I had been quick to realize that my father drank. Meals took place in silence; once or twice my father started off on a confused story that I had trouble following, and that my mother would listen to without saying a word. He used to break off before getting to the point.

When I had gone to my room after dinner, I frequently overheard noisy and, to me, unintelligible scenes, which gave me the feeling that I ought to go to my mother's aid. From where I lay in bed I would listen as voices rose above sounds of overturning furniture. Sometimes I got up and, posted in the hallway, waited until things quietened down. Once the door opened; I caught sight of my father, red-faced, swaying, like a drunk from the slums, a strange sight in the opulent setting of the house. Whenever he spoke to me it was always with a kind of tenderness, with inept, shaky, almost boyishly clumsy gestures. It terrified me. Another time I came upon him rushing about the drawing-room; he was bumping into chairs and chasing my half-undressed mother; he himself was in a nightshirt. He caught up with her; together they fell to the floor, yelling. I stole off and realized then that I should have stayed out of the way. One fine day he opened the door to my room by mistake; he swayed on the threshold, a bottle in his hand; noticing me, he let go of it, and liquor flowed from the broken glass. For a moment I gazed at him; he clutched his head after the bottle made its awful smashing sound, he kept still, but I trembled.

I detested him so heartily that I took the opposite view to his on everything. At that stage I had become devout to the point of imagining myself eventually entering the Church. My father was then ardently anti-clerical. Not until he was dead did I decide against a religious vocation in order to live with my mother, before whom I stood in blind adoration. I believed that my mother was what, in my foolishness, I supposed all women were, I believed that she was what only male vanity could prevent a person from being, attached to

religion. Did I not go with her to Mass on Sunday? My mother
loved me; I believed that we thought and felt alike, in a unison
marred only by the presence of the intruder, my father. True,
she was constantly going out of the house; it was a source of
unhappiness for me, but how could I disapprove of any
attempt on her part to get away from that loathsome
individual?

To be sure, she continued to go out during my father's
absences, and I wondered at that. He often went for lengthy
stays in Nice, and there I knew he had the time of his life,
gambling and drinking as usual. Learning of his imminent
departure I would be tempted to tell my mother how
overjoyed I felt; she, curiously downcast, would avoid
conversation, but I was sure she was no less happy than I. His
last trip was to Brittany, where he had been invited by his
sister; my mother was to have accompanied him but at the last
minute she decided to remain at home. At dinner, with my
father gone, I was in such high spirits that I dared tell my
mother how thrilled I was to be alone with her; to my surprise
she seemed greatly pleased by what I said, although her
response was more light-headed than sensible.

I had grown a lot by that time. All of a sudden I had turned
into a man; she promised we would go out together to a fine
restaurant.

'I look young enough to reflect well on you,' she told me.
'But you are such a handsome creature they'll take you for my
lover.'

I laughed, for she was laughing, but it had fairly staggered
me. I could not believe my mother had uttered the word. It
seemed to me she had been drinking.

Up till then I had never noticed that she drank. I was soon to
realize that she drank every day, in the same way. But that
rippling laughter, that indecent exuberance; she was not

always like that. Rather, she would be sad, appealingly mild; she would seal herself up; she had a deep melancholy I blamed on my father's wickedness, and that melancholy was what decided my lifelong dedication.

After dessert she went off and I remained behind, disappointed. Did she so much as care if I was vexed? My disappointment lasted through the following days. My mother never stopped laughing — and drinking — and above all going away. I stayed by myself and worked. I was at school at the time, I was studying, and, like someone who has taken to drink, I drowned myself in work.

One day my mother did not leave the house after lunch as she cutomarily did. She laughed with me. She apologized for not having kept her promise, for not having taken me out 'to wine and dine together', as she put it. My mother, previously so grave, at the sight of whom one felt a tugging uneasiness, the feeling one has on the eve of a storm, suddenly appeared to me in a new light: that of a young scatterbrain. I knew she was beautiful: for years I had been hearing people say so. But this provocative coquetry in her was new to me. She was thirty-two and, as I stared at her, her elegance and her manner overwhelmed me.

'I'm taking you to town tomorrow,' she said. 'There's a kiss for you, until tomorrow night, mv gallant lover!'

Whereupon she laughed unrestrainedly, put on her hat, her gloves, and so to speak slipped away from between my fingers.

When she had left I told myself that her beauty, her laugh, were diabolical.

My mother was not in the house for dinner that evening. I had an early class the next day; my mind was on my schoolwork as I made my way home. When she let me in the maid said my mother was in her room waiting for me. Her expression was dark. Right away she said, 'I have bad news about your father.'

I stood still and listened.

'It was sudden,' she said.

'He's dead?' I asked.

'Yes,' she said.

She was silent for a while. Then she went on, 'We are going to Vannes by train. From Vannes station we shall take a carriage to Segrais.'

I simply asked what my father had so suddenly died from. She answered me and then stood up. She made a helpless gesture. She was tired, a weight seemed to lie upon her shoulders, but of her feelings she said nothing apart from this: 'If you speak to Robert or Marthe don't forget that you are supposed to be borne down by grief. Our good servants consider that we ought to be in tears. There's no need to weep, but lower your eyes.'

My equanimity, I could see, was irritating my mother, whose voice had sharpened. My gaze remained fastened upon her. I was startled to see that she had aged. I was startled and bewildered. Could I conceal the pious jubilation which was winning out inside me against the conventional sorrow that is bound up with the sly advent of death? I did not want my mother to age, I wanted to see her set free, freed from her oppressor and also from the mad gaiety she took refuge in and which made her face lie. I wanted to be happy, I even wanted this bereavement in which fate was enfolding us to flavour our happiness with the spellbinding sadness that makes up the sweetness of death.

But I bent my head; my mother's phrase caused me more than shame. I felt cut. I thought that I was going to cry, at least as much from resentment as from a ludicrous anger. And since death calls for the most stupid tears anyhow, when I spoke to the servants of our misfortune, I wept.

The clatter of the carriage, then that of the train, fortunately kept us silent. I fell into a doze and it enabled me to forget.

My one concern was to avoid getting on my mother's nerves

again. However, I risked the suggestion that we stop
overnight in a hotel in Vannes before going on. She must have
telegraphed ahead that we would be arriving the next day, for,
without saying anything, she went along with my idea. In the
restaurant and afterwards at the station we did at last begin to
talk about this and that. Do what I could, my awkwardness
and my immaturity were making themselves felt. I failed to
notice at first that my mother was drinking; but I understood
when she called for a second bottle. Alarmed, I looked down
at my plate; when I raised my eyes I met my mother's gaze,
and its hardness shook me. She filled her glass ostentatiously.
She sat waiting for the damnable moment my foolishness was
heading us towards.

In that gaze, heavy with fatigue, there shone a tear.

She wept and tears glided down her cheeks.

'Mother,' I said, 'isn't it better for him? And for you too?'

'Be quiet,' she snapped.

With me she was all hostility, as though venting her hatred.

I stumbled on, 'Mother, you know anyway that for him it's
better.'

She was drinking fast. A queer smile came upon her face.

'Say it: I made his life hell.'

I was perplexed and I protested. 'He is dead and we
shouldn't say anything against him. But your life was
difficult.'

'What do you know about it?' she retorted.

The smile had not gone away. For her I had ceased to exist.

'You know nothing about my life.'

She meant to go the whole way. The second bottle was
empty already.

The waiter came up, served us. The odour in the restaurant
was of staleness, degrading, the tablecloth was spotted with
red. The air was sultry.

'Feels like a storm coming up,' the waiter remarked.

Nobody responded.

How, I asked myself, trembling opposite my mother, how
could I blame her? And I was mortified to have doubted her

even for an instant. I flushed, I wiped beads of sweat from my forehead.

My mother was by now completely withdrawn, remote. But suddenly the hardness vanished from her features; the way wax melts, they softened, for an instant she drew in her lower lip.

'Pierre,' she said, 'look at me.'

That mobile, that fugitive countenance grew overcast: a look of horror possessed it. She fought against the dizziness mounting in her. She spoke carefully, slowly, her features frozen, gripped by an insanity.

What my mother said tortured me. Her solemnity and, more than that, more terrible than that, her hideous grandeur preyed upon me. I listened, prostrated.

'You are too young,' said she, 'I oughtn't to talk to you at all, but sooner or later you will be wondering whether your mother merits your respect. Well, your father is dead now and I am tired of falsehoods: I am worse than he.'

She smiled a bitter smile that was no smile at all. With both hands she caught at the neck of her dress and drew it open; there was no indecency in the gesture, it simply expressed an agony.

'Pierre,' she went on, 'you alone have any respect for your mother, who deserves none. The men you saw in the drawing-room one day, those pretty fops, just who do you fancy they were?'

I didn't answer. I hadn't paid any attention.

'As for your father, he knew. Your father went along with it. Once you were gone those idiots stopped having a respectful attitude towards your mother. Look at her!'

Her hideous, distraught smile was the smile of woe.

My mother loved me: was it really in her power to put up with the innocent foolishness to which my piety — and her lies — had reduced me?

Later she was to borrow a phrase from my father, 'Just lay

the blame for everything on me.' That was his wish, understanding that in my eyes my mother was beyond reproach and must at all costs remain that way. But perpetuating that convention became intolerable after his death. And in the upheaval which followed it she yielded to the temptation to display her awfulness to me, as she liked to do every time she lost her grip.

'What I want', were the words she left me with, administering a poison, 'is that you love me even unto death. For my part, it is in death I love you at this very instant. But I don't want your love unless you know I am repulsive, and love me even as you know it.'

Shattered, I left the hotel dining-room and went upstairs, choking on my tears.

At the open window, looking out at the stormy sky, I listened for a moment to the hissing, the whistling and panting of steam engines. I stood and addressed that God who tore at me, within my heart, and whom that heart, bursting, could not contain. In my anguish I felt emptiness invading me. Me, I was too puny, too pitiable. I was no match for what was besetting me, for the horror. I heard thunder boom. I subsided upon the rug. After a while I got the idea of turning over and lying flat and spreading out my arms, like a suppliant.

Much later I heard my mother enter her room. Between it and mine was a communicating door which I remembered having left ajar. I heard footsteps approach and the door quietly pulled shut. The closing of the door restored me to solitude, but I had the feeling that nothing would ever be able to help me back out of it, and I remained on the floor, letting my tears flow in silence.

The continued rolling of thunder did not prevent me from sinking towards sleep. The sudden opening of the door coincided with the fierce flash of lightning which had started me awake; rain was splashing down in torrents. I heard my mother moving barefoot inside my room. She paused, but I did not have time enough to get up. Finding I was not in my bed, not seeing me anywhere else in the room, she called my name.

Then she stumbled over me. I rose. I took her in my arms. We were both afraid, we were weeping. We covered each other with kisses. Her nightgown had slipped off her shoulders so that the body I hugged was halfway naked. A patch of rain blown in through the window had drenched her; reeling, her hair unloosened, she spoke without knowing what she was saying.

And in the meantime I helped her to a chair.

She went on talking, raving; but, the nightgown back where it belonged, she was decent again. Through her tears she smiled at me, but unhappiness had got into her like a cramp and, bent over, she clutched herself as though about to have to vomit.

'You have turned out to be nice,' she said. 'I deserved something else. I should have found myself with some buck who would have abused me. I'd have preferred that. The gutter, the dungheap, that's where your mother feels at home. You shall never know what horrors I am capable of. I'd like you to know, though. I like my filth. Today I'll end up being sick, I have had too much to drink, I'd feel better if I threw up. Even if I did my worst in front of you I'd still be pure in your eyes.'

Then she brought out that smutty laugh, the sound of which has left me impaired like a cracked bell.

I was standing up, my shoulders and head drooping.

My mother had got to her feet, she started towards her room. Another laugh that rang false; but she turned around and, although her step was uncertain, she took me by the shoulders and she said, 'Forgive me.' Then, lowering her voice, 'You must forgive me: I am disgusting and I have had a lot to drink. But I love you and respect you and I couldn't stand to go on lying. Yes, your mother is revolting, and to overcome your revulsion you will have to be very strong.'

Finally, and it was after a struggle, she brought out the rest almost in a gasp. 'I could have spared you all this, gone on lying, I could have treated you like a simpleton. I am an evil woman, I am rotten and I drink, but you are not a coward. It took courage to tell you what I did. Think of that. If I've been drinking all night it's because I needed help and perhaps it was to help you. So now help me, take me into my room and lay me down to sleep.'

It was a worn-out old woman I saw to her bed that night. And afterwards I found myself alone, dazed, tottering, in an icy world. Had I been able to, I would have been quite willing to die.

My father's funeral, proceeding from the family's house to the church, then to the Segrais graveyard — I remember all that as a kind of gap in time, empty for want of substance. My mother, swathed in mourning, and the falsehood of the priests, who, since it was an unbeliever they were burying, were not supposed to chant . . . Well, none of it mattered, and my mother's veils which, owing to the ungodly things they veiled, simply — despite myself — made me want to laugh, they didn't matter to me either. I was inwardly in shreds. I was losing my wits.

For I had understood that malediction, terror, sown in me like seed, now belonged to my flesh. The death of my father, I had thought, was going to restore me to life, but this semblance of life inside my black clothing was now making me tremble. Everything within me was a stabbing confusion, and nothing else from now on held any interest for me. In the profoundness of my indifference I felt myself similar to God. In this lifeless world what else was there for me to do but forget the searing light whose glare had blinded me when I had felt my mother in my arms? But I already knew that it was not going to be forgotten, ever.

In the solitude I entered, the norms of this world, if they subsist, do so in order to maintain a dizzying feeling of enormity: this solitude, it is God.

My distress was so great that I went to bed as soon as we returned from Segrais, claiming I was sick. The doctor was called, he examined me. My mother came into my room, and the doctor's 'Nothing very serious', and the shrug accompanying his verdict, cleared my health. All the same, I stayed in bed, my meals were brought to my room.

Then I told myself that I'd only gain a small amount of time by persisting on this tack. I dressed and knocked at my mother's door.

'I'm not sick,' I told her.

'No, I knew you weren't,' she said.

I tried to outstare her, but in her eyes I encountered an anger and a hostility which terrified me.

'I am getting up now. I'll have lunch in the dining-room, if that's all right.'

She contemplated me. Her perfect dignity, her composure were a very poor response to all that I was feeling. But, linked to that smouldering threat of outburst which exalted her, there burned in her an intolerable scorn for me.

At Vannes she had wanted to shame herself and now, no doubt, she was making it up to herself. But on more than one occasion was I to measure the supreme contempt she could have for those who failed to accept her as she was.

Impatience showed behind that flawless calm. 'It is good to

see you again, Pierre. According to the doctor there is nothing wrong with you; but I knew that. I told you so before; you'll not surmount anything by running away. And first of all that means stopping running away from me. I know that you still feel a deep respect for me, but I will not have some sort of madness getting in between the two of us. I would ask you to go on respecting me as fully as ever in the past. You must remain the submissive son of the woman of whose unworthiness you are aware.'

'I was afraid you'd take my uneasiness before you as a sign of disrespect. I am weak. I am unhappy. I can't even think any more.' By then I had tears in my eyes. 'Unhappy,' I went on, 'there's more to it than that. I am afraid.'

Her response was in the same harsh key, it contained the same note of hostility that had struck me when I'd first come into her room; and in it was the same element of suffering.

'You are right to be. But your one chance lies in facing up to what frightens you. You shall get back to your lessons. First, though, you are going to help me. Your father left a mess in the house, I would like you to pull yourself together and tidy up the chaos in his study, there are books and papers to sort through and arrange; I haven't the energy to take on the job myself and I don't want things left unattended any longer. Furthermore, I have to go out.'

She asked me to kiss her.

She was flushed. Her cheeks were burning.

With me looking on she carefully put on her hat, to which a widow's veil was pinned. Observing her, I saw that she was made up, that she was in an evening gown, that mourning indecently emphasized her beauty.

'I know just what you are thinking,' she added. 'From now on I am not going to spare you, I've decided that. I'll not change my desires. You shall respect me such as I am; I am not going to hide anything of myself from you. No more pretences: that at last is over with, and I am glad.'

'Nothing,' I answered her fervently, 'nothing you could do

would alter the respect I have for you. Saying so may be making me tremble; but you know I say it with all the strength there is in me.'

As for the haste with which she left, I could not tell whether it was due to eagerness for what she was going out to seek or because my loving behaviour had roused regrets in her. I did not as yet have any idea of the extent of the ravages addiction to pleasure had wrought in her heart. But from then on it was a vicious circle. It was harder than ever to become indignant about it; in fact, I never ceased to worship my mother, to venerate her as a saint. I might admit that all basis for that veneration was gone; I was none the less unable to refrain from it. And so I lived in an unappeasable torment from which only death and the crowning misfortune could release me. If I gave way to horror at the thought of the debauchery I now knew was the delight of my mother's life, then the respect I had for her would immediately make of me, and not of her, an object of horror. And, no sooner returned to my worshipful attitude, I would be forced to the realization that her debauchery nauseated me.

But that day when she went out, and when I ought to have realized where she was going in such a hurry, I had no inkling of the deadly snare she had set for me. I understood much later. Then, sunk to the depths of corruption and terror, I loved her unremittingly; I entered that delirium where it seemed to me I was lost in God.

I was in my father's study; a hateful disorder reigned there. The recollection of his insignificance, of his inanity, of his pretentiousness, stifled me. I did not yet have a feeling of what in all likelihood he had actually been: a buffoon, full of unexpectedly winning traits and of perverted whimsies, but charming at all times, always ready to give what he had.

I was the result of an affair he had had with my mother prior to their marriage, when she was fourteen. The family had been obliged to marry the two young monsters and the little monster had grown up amidst the chaos that permanently

characterized their home. Their wealth had provided for a
good many things, but in my father's library nothing had kept
the mess within bounds, a mess to which death had supplied
the finishing touches, consigning it to dust. Never had I seen
that room in such a state. Advertisements which had come in
the post, or heaps of scribbled accounts, medicine bottles,
grey bowlers, gloves, many buttons, more bottles and dirty
combs were mixed in amongst books of the widest variety and
of no interest whatsoever. I opened the shutters and rays of
sunshine brought moths fluttering out of the felt of the hats. I
decided to tell my mother that nothing short of a rigorous
sweeping out with a broom could set to rights a place filled
with rubbish existing for the sole purpose of disorder, but
before saying anything I thought I ought to take a thorough
look about. I felt I had to save any objects of value if there were
any to set aside. I did in fact find a few very handsome books. I
removed them from the shelves; that brought the books next
to them spilling out, and in the further jumble and the clouds
of extra dust I created my spirits sank near to collapse. It was
then that I made an unusual discovery. Lodged behind the
books, in the glass-fronted bookcases my father had kept
locked but to which my mother had given me the keys, I came
upon a heap of photographs. Most of them were dusty. But in
an instant I saw that they were incredibly obscene. I
reddened, I clenched my teeth and I was obliged to sit down,
but I still had a sheaf of those repulsive pictures in my hand.
My impulse was to rush out of there, but I had to do
something with them, to get rid of them before my mother's
return. Feverishly, I stacked them, made them into piles.
Upon the tables where I put them I piled them too high, they
fell, I surveyed the disaster: scattered by the dozen, those
pictures lay strewn upon the carpet, unspeakable and at the
same time compelling. Could I have fought against that rising
tide? From the first I had sensed that inward upheaval,
involuntary and burning, which had made me despair when
my half-naked mother had flung herself into my arms. I

looked at those pictures and trembled but I made the trembling last. I lost control and helplessly sent the remaining piles flying. But I had to pick them back up . . . My father, my mother and this swamp of obscenity . . . out of despair I decided to follow this horror through. I stared down at what I was already grasping in my hand, like an ape; I wrapped myself in the dust and took off my trousers.

Interwoven joy and terror strangled me within. I strangled and I gasped from pleasure. The more those pictures terrified me, the more intense was my excitement at the sight of them. After days of accumulating alarms, tensions, suffocations, I was beyond withstanding my own ignominy. I invoked it and I blessed it. It was my inevitable fate: my joy was all the greater since, with regard to life, I had long since entrenched myself in an attitude of suffering, and now, in the throes of delight, I progressed even farther into vileness and degradation. I sensed that I was damned, I defiled myself before the filth in which my father — and perhaps my mother too — had wallowed. It well became the swine I was going to turn into, born of the coupling of the boar and the sow.

Inherent in motherhood, I told myself, is the doing of that which in children causes these terrible convulsions.

That multitude of lewd images spread out before me over the floor.

Tall men with thick moustaches and wearing garters and women's striped stockings* lunged at other men or at girls, some of whom were stout and whose figures repelled me. But certain of them, most of them in fact, delighted me: their repulsive postures quickened my delight. In that state of

* Sometimes the stockings were striped horizontally, sometimes vertically. The daring, obscene photographs of the period resorted to these odd devices, striving for a comic and unpleasant quality through which they obtained a maximum effectiveness — a maximum shamefulness.

impending spasm and woe, one of these creatures, whose picture I had in my hand (stretched out on the carpet, leaning upon one elbow, I was in pain and the dust had dirtied me) appeared to me of such beauty (she was underneath a man, lying on her back, her head thrown back and her stricken eyes wandering) that the phrase 'the beauty of death' crossing my mind, the words imposing themselves on my mind, brought on the clinging shudder and, as I locked my teeth, the decision — or what I believed was my decision — to kill myself.

A long while I remained upon the floor, inert, half-naked, obscene, surrounded by images of obscenity. I dozed off.

Night fell and my mother rapped at the door.

Panic seized me. I called out, saying I would be there in a minute. Readjusting my clothing, I collected the photographs together as best, as rapidly, as I could, I thrust them out of sight, then I opened the door for my mother, who switched on the light.

'I'd fallen asleep,' I explained.

I was utterly deplorable.

It was a nightmare, worse than any I can remember. My one hope was to not survive it. My mother herself, plainly, had received a fright. Today, the only memory I can still associate with that situation is of teeth chattering in high fever. Much later, my mother admitted that it had been a shock, that she had sensed that she had gone too far. She was consistent, however: imagining a suicide, mistakenly, as it turned out, she could then — and what else could she do? — tell herself she had been frightened all along by the monstrous desire which had given her the idea of having me tidy the library. For she herself had tried to do the job, had been revolted, had sadistically decided to entrust it to me. Whereupon she had sailed out to her frolics.

She loved me, her wish had been to keep me away from calamity and the terrible joys she found there; but I, had I resisted the inspirations of horror? Those joys were now known to me; and, despite her best intentions, it had been as though she could not rest until she had somehow got me to share in that for which a mutual disgust drove her to ecstasy.

Opposite me — like me — she was in the grip of excitement. From that excitement she was able to derive a strange calm, and, after a long while, she said, calmly, in a tone that was warm and whose charm was soothing, 'Come to my room. I do not want to leave you by yourself. Do as I say. If you lack pity for yourself, I ask you to be merciful with me. But if that is what you'd like, I shall be strong enough for two.'

After my long distress that voice brought me back to life. It cheered me, I cherished it, the more so because, knowing what I did, I had been ready to think that everything would be lost, while now all of a sudden I felt this unshakeable serenity, proof against the worst, resurging intact out of infamy.

She went first, I followed her into the bedroom where I dropped on the chair she had asked me to take.

Just as I was leaving the library I had seen, still lying on the floor, some photographs which in my haste I had overlooked. I was relieved to have seen them, to know that there could be no possibility of doubt. It was a relief for me to be able to share the shame I supposed my mother must feel before me, who knew of her abjection; I was grateful to be able to think of myself as more thoroughly shameful than she. In the acceptance of my downfall, I descended to the level where — if I was to survive — my life was henceforth due to drag itself out. Now, in my defeated eyes, my mother could read my ignominy. It nauseated me but I preferred that she should know I had lost the right — which I would never ever have invoked — to blush on her account. No more would she sense a virtuousness in me because of which her weakness could become detestable and the gulf between herself and me wider. I just had to grow accustomed to the idea of being from now on someone without substance; in that way I would attain the only thing which in the light of my longings was from now on worth having; even if it made me dreadfully unhappy, and even if it were to remain for ever unspoken, all I wanted was for a feeling of complicity to unite us, my mother and I.

I lingered over these and similar thoughts, vainly seeking something to hold on to, as though there were still the barest chance of finding a way to halt on that slope I had begun to head down.

In my mother's facial expression there had always been a strange, incomprehensible element: a kind of incipient bad temper, a crossness which stood close to gaiety but sometimes veered towards provocation, towards the flaunting of ignominy. With me she now had an absent air, and yet I could sense the outburst gathering in her, an insane outburst of gaiety or shameless provocation, as at the theatre one may sense that there are actors in the wings ready to pop out on to the stage at any moment.

There may also have been something illusory in this anticipation of the impossible that my mother often aroused in me. For her voice, which rarely lost its captivating distinction and evenness, did not take long to undermine that anticipation, transforming it into appeasement. This time it woke me from the aching dream in which life seemed about to fade away altogether.

'I owe you no explanations,' she began. 'But in Vannes I'd drunk unreasonably. I ask you to forget it.

'Understand me,' she continued. 'You are not to forget what I said. But I wouldn't have had the strength to say it, had your childishness — and what I was drinking — and perhaps grief not upset my bearings.'

She paused, waiting, I thought, for some reply from me; but I lowered my head. She resumed.

'I would like to talk to you *now*. I am not sure of helping you, but better that you be brought down still further than abandoned to the solitude in which I fear you are enclosing yourself. I know you are atrociously unhappy. You are weak, you too. Your father was weak the way you are. After the other day you know how far my weakness goes. You perhaps now know that desire reduces us to pulp. But you do not yet know what I know.'

From somewhere, somehow, I found the audacity — the simplicity — to say, 'I would like to know what you know.'

'No, Pierre,' she said, 'you must not learn it from me. But you would pardon me if you knew. You would even excuse your father. And above all. . .'

I looked at her.

'You would forgive yourself.'

For a long moment I remained still.

'Now,' my mother said, 'you must start living.'

While speaking she had dropped her gaze and her wonderful countenance was inscrutable. Then I saw a perfectly ordinary little smile appear there.

'You are not very cheerful,' she remarked.

I said nothing.

'Neither am I.'

It was time to sit down at table. She insisted that I talk to her about my schoolwork. Just as if nothing had happened.

I talked about it.

When my mother had once more gone out, I found myself lying in bed. Amidst those depraved imaginings in which we often indulge against our will, I thought of her gone in pursuit of pleasure. But before leaving the house she had come into my room to tuck me in, as she used to do when I was a little boy. Not once during the whole of that day had I thought of how she had deliberately exposed me to the incitations of the photographs. I lived suspended in admiration, fascinated by the affectionate sweetness that alternated in her with fits of derangement: breakdowns of which she seemed to me to be the victim and which, I could see, made her unhappy, as I was

unhappy because of what, that afternoon, had befallen me
without my wanting it. Tucked in by her, I rested in bed, like
the victim after his accident. Someone who has sustained a
serious injury, who is in pain and has lost a lot of blood, must
have, I imagine, feelings similar to what mine were, if at last
he wakes up again in his bandages, but in the peaceful
surroundings of the nursing-home.

God is the dread in me of what was, of what is, of what will be so horrible that I must deny at all costs and with all my strength cry my denial that that was, that that is, or that that will be, but I shall be lying.

Life got started again. Slow-moving time healed the gash. To me my mother seemed calm, I admired, I loved her self-mastery, that coolness had a profoundly soothing effect upon me. Never had I loved her more. Never had my devotion to her been so great, the more so and the madder for the fact that, united now in the same malediction, we were divorced from the rest of the world. Between her and me a new bond had formed; moral decline and cowardice were its sinews. Far from regretting having succumbed in my turn, I saw that my *sin* had given me access to what appeared to me my mother's misfortune, which must eventually lay her low as it was laying me low, but which, I later understood, by torturing us, provided it tortured us, was to prepare us for the one happiness that is not meaningless, since we become its prey when in the grip of misfortune.

But at the outset I could not accept this secret marriage of heaven and hell. It was, after all, painful to feel that my mother delighted in the misery I knew she was condemned to. Every evening, and sometimes in the afternoon also, she would go out. When she dined at home I usually noticed signs she had been drinking. I said nothing, I waited, to surrender to my grief, until she had gone out again, until she had returned to her swill. I recalled the time when I deplored my father's boozing, when my mother's silence and gravity allowed me to believe that she shared my attitude. And now I realized that she used to drink at the same time as my father, if not together with him. (But she had always maintained a dignity he never had; it had hardly ever deserted her, except at Vannes.) The most stupid part is that, notwithstanding the evidence, I went right on accusing my father and him alone. My father, whose impudence told of an appalling inner confusion, my father who, I was sure of it, had got my mother into the habit of drinking and had finally managed to corrupt her, my father whose filth had, after his death, warped me in my turn.

Tooth and nail I fought against recognition of the truth which later on, before dying, my mother forced me to see: that at the age of fourteen she had chased after my father; and when the pregnancy that resulted in me obliged the family to marry them, it was she who went from debauch to debauch, corrupting him through and through with the same shrewd obstinacy she was to demonstrate with me. If ultimately there was a tantalizing rectitude about her, she was none the less cunning: her exceeding gentleness, howbeit mitigated sometimes by the disturbing oppressiveness that foretells a storm in the air, left me utterly blind. I lived with the feeling that a hidden leprosy was gnawing our vitals: of this ill we were never to be cured, by this malady we were both mortally afflicted. My childish imagination dwelled fixedly upon the evidence of a calamity that my mother and I were undergoing jointly.

   Yet this wreck did not proceed without my active consent. I made myself cosily at home in the certitude of inevitable disaster. One day I took advantage of my mother's absence and relapsed. Wrung by temptation, I entered the library and first drew out a couple of photographs, soon two others, and slowly my head began to spin. I enjoyed the innocence of unhappiness and of helplessness; could I blame myself for a sin which attracted me, which flooded me with pleasure precisely to the extent it brought me to despair?

I doubted, I hovered in permanent anguish and, in my anguish, I yielded over and over again to the desire to be the object of my own horror. I thought continually of the confession I ought to make of my baseness, but it was not just owning to an unspeakable depravity that frightened me, to me the idea of confession seemed more and more a betrayal of my mother, a severing of that ineluctable tie which our common ignominy had created between us. True baseness, so I thought, would be to tell my confessor, who knew my mother, and who, along with me, considered that all the wickedness lay with my father, that now I *loved* my mother's sins and that I was as proud of them as a savage. I knew in advance just what language the priest would employ. His banal exhortations, what sense would they make when my distress was so great, so irremediable the situation in which God's wrath had placed me?

For me, only my mother's gentle — and always tragic — phrases were appropriate to a drama, a mystery, which was no less grave, no less dazzling than God himself. It seemed to me that my mother's monstrous impurity, and mine, no less revolting, cried out to heaven and that they bore an affinity to God, inasmuch as only utter darkness can be likened to light. I remembered La Rochefoucauld's terse line, 'The eye can outstare neither the sun nor death.' Death, in my eyes, was no less divine than the sun, and in her crimes my mother was nearer to God than anything I had perceived through the window of the Church. Again and again during those interminable days of my solitude and of my sinfulness I would stiffen as though from an electric shock when the thought thrilled through me that my mother's crime elevated her into God, in the very way in which terror and the vertiginous idea of God became identified. And, wanting to find God, I wanted to burrow down and cover myself with mud, so as not to be more unworthy of Him than my mother. The ignominious scenes shown in the photographs in my eyes acquired that brilliance and that grandeur but for which life would be without rapture and its eye never turned upon the sun or upon death.

Little did they matter to me, those feelings I had of having sunk below the human as I peered at myself and, in the dark rings under my eyes, saw the reflection of my fall. That fall brought me nearer to my mother's nakedness, to the hell where she had elected to live — or rather to cease to breathe, to stop living. Sometimes I would select the most sickening of my father's pictures, I would undress and I would cry out, 'God of terror, very low dost thou bring us, very low hast thou brought us, my mother and me . . .' I realized in the course of time that I took pride in being like this, and, reminding myself that pride was the worst sin of all, I would straighten up. For I knew that the seemliness I saw represented by my confessor would have been, for me, the negation of that God of blinding sunlight, of that God of death I was seeking, towards whom I was being guided along the unhappy paths my mother traced.

Then I recalled my father, his drunkard side. I had cursed him unthinkingly, now at last I began to doubt my right to do so: through him I belonged to drunkenness and aberration, to everything bad that the world contains, from even the very worst of which God never turns his face away. My father, that dead-drunk clown the police sometimes picked up out of the gutter, the thought of my father suddenly touched me to tears. I remembered the night at the station in Vannes and the alternative to my mother's moments of desperate calm, suddenly remembering the smile that stole over her face, which deformed her features, as if they had melted and run.

I would tremble and I was unhappy, but I enjoyed opening myself to all the world's disorder. Could I have avoided succumbing to evil, to the malady which was choking my mother? For several days she was away from the house. I spent my time destroying myself — or weeping: waiting for her.

Laughter is more divine and in meaning
more elusive than tears.

When she returned home my mother noticed my sunken eyes. She smiled.

'We shall take care of that,' she said. 'Tonight I feel worn to pieces, I am going to bed.'

'We look a little alike, Mother. Look in the mirror, the rings under those eyes.'

'It's true, upon my soul,' she said. 'I prefer your malice to your bedraggled appearance.'

With that she laughed and gave me a kiss.

When next we met it was at breakfast the following day.

'Why, it's getting worse by the minute,' she declared, 'something must be done for my Pierre right away. Do you know what Rhea calls you?'

'Rhea?'

'That's so, you haven't really met her yet. You passed one another on the stairs. She's a very pretty girl, but pretty girls apparently scare you. Rhea saw you well enough, she at once recognized the handsome boy I sometimes talk to her about. She asked after you the other day, "How is our Knight of the Sorrowful Countenance?" It's time you led a less secluded life, in my opinion. Ordinarily a boy of your age goes out and meets women. Tonight we are going to go out with Rhea. I'll not be in mourning, and you'll dress up in your best. I mustn't forget: Rhea is a great friend of mine; she is adorable, she is a professional dancer, she is the most wonderfully crazy girl in the whole world. I'll bring her back with me at five so that the two of you can get acquainted this afternoon, if you like. Before going out to dinner we'll have some refreshments at home.' She had spoken softly, modulating her phrases; and now she laughed sweetly.

'Yes, Mother,' I stammered.

I was flabbergasted. I told myself that she wore that smile like a mask.

At this point my mother rose. We went to the table.

'I wouldn't call that a very hearty response. Where wickedness is needed, I'm plainly going to have to supply enough for both of us.'

Again she laughed. But the sad truth — that I loved — continued to proclaim itself, behind the mask.

'Mother!' I cried.

'Your mother,' she said, 'will have to be a bit rougher with you.'

Reaching forward, she pinched my cheeks.

'Show your mettle.'

I considered her.

'There's more to it than loving one's mother, being intelligent, being handsome and being so deeply serious. It's worrying. Where will this seriousness get you if it shuts out the gaiety of others?'

I was thinking of crime, I was thinking of death. I put my hands up to my face.

'You are serious too.'

'Great silly! Will you just look at him! Without your playfulness you'd be all dullness.'

The system I had built up, within which I had taken refuge, was now about to collapse. My mother might sometimes be in a jovial humour, but there was always a catch to that gaiety of hers, a barb to her playfulness.

During the meal she remained in high spirits, teasing me for my sobriety or making me laugh in spite of myself.

'You see', she said, 'what can happen to me without even a drop to drink. You can be proud of your profundity, it's put me in this wonderful mood! Tell me now, joking aside: are you afraid?'

'Why . . . no.'

'A pity.'

Yet again she laughed, then left.

I stayed on in the dining-room;-I sat in the corner with my head bowed.

I would obey, I knew it in advance. I would even contrive to show my mother that she was wrong to make fun of me. When called upon I too would give proof of playfulness, of this I was only too sure. At that point it occurred to me that if I could put on a show of easy behaviour, then perhaps my mother might also have been feigning something she did not truly feel. This notion enabled me to preserve intact the whole edifice of ideas in which I wanted to remain entrenched. By doing so I could respond to the inducements of my fate, which invited me to sink incessantly lower, to go whither my mother was enticing me and to drink my cup with her, drink it the moment she wanted me to, to the dregs . . . Her playfulness dazzled me, but must I not all the same see that by rendering me carefree, it was the surest means to speed me towards my desired destination, the heart of danger, the vortex of joy? Did I not know that in the end my mother would take me to where she was going? Ever my seductress, the means she now meant to use were infernal debauches, infernal especially because of her seeming dignity. And just as my mother was perpetually fluctuating between brazen disgrace and splendour, amourousness and gravity, so confusion invaded my mind before the uncertain prospect which Rhea's imaginable levity made upsetting. My mother wishes to have me meet her friend, I said to myself, but am I not mad to leap to the conclusion that she has asked this friend of hers to be my undoing? But, I immediately conjectured, what dancer who was a close friend of hers could help but be party to her wild carrying on?

It was in that fever of suspense I waited. I was drawn to Rhea beforehand. More than drawn to her, I was fascinated by her, this Rhea who could be my introduction into the world which terrified me but which, in my terror, was the subject of all my thoughts.

Those were unhappy thoughts, but the menace they conveyed was that of an excessive joy, which my terror was going to give birth to; the fantastic image I conceived of Rhea thus combined with everything else to unsettle me altogether. I raved; I could see her taking off her clothes at the very first word; her sluttishness would force my mother to flee, I would be abandoned to this devil-fish who, all arms, all legs, resembled the whores my father's obscenities had furnished my imagination with. Childishly, I gave free rein to those reveries. I did not believe in them, but I was already so warped that I invented the most precisely detailed scenes in order to excite myself and, sensually, to wallow in a warmer mire of shame.

Today I find it hard to describe those febrile moments when along with revolt I was gripped by greed for a terrifying pleasure, a strangling pleasure, one which, the more it strangled me, the more it would overpower me. I think finally that it was a game I was playing, not only because of the cheating I resorted to but because of the skill and self-possession I displayed the moment any difficulty arose. I might feel paralysed when I entered the drawing room and when, against a background of rich draperies and tapestry, I beheld my mother and her friend, both dressed in red and their faces aglow; for an instant I lost my breath; I was already stunned, but with admiration. I went towards them, smiling. I met my mother's glance, read approval there. I had indeed dressed and got myself up with more than usual care. When I approached them I was not trembling. I kissed — even took my time kissing — the hand of the pretty Rhea, whose perfume, whose gown — whose sparkling eyes — affected me just as much, and just as intimately, as would have the enactment of the fantasies which had been tormenting me all afternoon.

'You will forgive me, Madame,' was my speech to Rhea, 'if I am — how shall I say? at a loss . . . But I am sure I would be still more awkward before you if I did not feel as though you belonged to another world . . .'

'Isn't he entertaining!' was Rhea's languid reply. 'So young, and already able to speak to women so well, to lie so nicely.'

Oh, there was no doubt, I was born for the world Rhea was opening up for me. But a sudden burst of laughter from my mother brought me up short, I heard her and I saw her; her presence, which for a brief instant I had forgotten, and that indecent laugh, were a shock. I suddenly felt terribly ill at ease.

'You will be cross,' said Rhea, 'but Pierre — allow me, dear, to call him by his first name — Pierre, I would be happier if you did not lie.'

Rhea seemed to have misunderstood, and this disconcerted me.

'Pierre,' my mother broke in, 'sit down here next to my friend. Unless I am mistaken, she is your friend too.'

She designated the spot I was to occupy on the sofa.

Two dissolute ladies in the company of a partner: it was exactly as I had imagined it. Rhea made room for me beside her. Then moved closer to me. And the champagne was flowing already, excitement was rising like the bubbles in the wine.

Rhea's dress, her neckline . . . I winced; I had reddened.

'But Pierre,' my neighbour was saying, 'don't you like having a good time? Your mother loves having a good time.'

'Madame — '

'To begin with, you must say "Rhea". Promise?'

She took my hand, then, having stroked it, placed it upon her leg. That was too much. Had I not been immobilized in that deep sofa I would certainly have attempted escape; but I would have fled weakly, and with the certainty of not getting far.

The tinge of affectation disappeared from Rhea's voice.

'It's true,' said she, 'I am on a spree but, you know, I've never regretted it, even though I come from a comfortably well-off family . . . You know, Pierre, there's no need for you to be afraid of women on a spree. Let your mother be better than we — '

'Better?' my mother interrupted. The mask of laughter set aside, she had suddenly turned back into what she was. 'Do you know anyone worse? I want Pierre to realize it.'

'Darling, you are distressing him, and why?'

'Rhea, I want to wake him up to the facts of life. Pour the champagne, Pierre.'

I picked up the bottle and I refilled the glasses, alarmed at the state my mother was working herself into. She was tall, slender, and all of a sudden she gave me the impression of being exhausted. Her eyes shone hatred and her features had already begun to blur.

'I want you to know it once and for all.'

She drew Rhea into her arms and kissed her straightway, convulsively.

'I am glad to be what I am!' she cried, addressing me. 'I want you to know it: I am the worst sort of mother.'

She put on a simpering grin.

'Hélène,' Rhea wailed, 'you are ghastly . . .'

I stood up.

'Pierre, listen to me,' my mother said (her calm had returned; her tone was crisp but grave and her sentences proceeded smoothly). 'It wasn't for that I asked you to be here today. But I do not want to have you hanging on to me any more. I want to see scorn in your eyes, scorn and fear. You see how easily I can forget your father. Learn from me that nothing incites one so much to wickedness as being happy.'

I was drunk; nevertheless I realized that my mother, who had been already drunk when I entered the drawing-room, no longer had the strength to keep on her feet.

'Mother,' I said, 'excuse me. I'd like to go to bed.'

'I'd not have thought', my mother began, her eyes oblivious to me, 'that my son would fail me on the very day he was to be witness to his mother's misbehaviour.' Then, with a naturalness which suddenly calmed me, brought me back to my senses, she said, 'Stay here, I love you with all my heart now that I have given you the right to see what I am made of.'

Her smile was the rueful, the artless smile I was so familiar with by now: the smile that went with a biting of her lip.

'Hélène!' Rhea protested, plainly disappointed.

She stood up.

'Don't you want to have dinner with him, darling? You want to nip straight into bed with him, is that it?'

Rhea touched her lips gently to mine. She looked as though she was getting ready to leave. I was stunned. I was utterly drunk.

My mother stood up too. She was glaring at Rhea; in another instant, I thought, she would be at her throat.

'Come here,' she ordered her.

Seizing her by the wrist, she led Rhea into the next room. I wasn't able to see them, but they were not far away; I would have been able to hear their movements had not the champagne then sent me off to sleep.

When I opened my eyes I found my mother gazing at me, a champagne glass in her hand,

Rhea also was gazing at me.

'We have shining eyes,' said my mother.

Rhea laughed. I saw her eyes shine.

'Let's be off, the driver is waiting,' my mother said.

'First, though,' said Rhea, 'let's brighten that sorrowful countenance.'

'And there's still some left in the bottle,' said my mother, 'take your glass, give us something to drink.'

'Everyone, up with your glass,' said Rhea, 'and cheers.'

A wave of merriment swept over us. I suddenly reached towards Rhea, I kissed her hard.

Out we went and down the stairs, quickly. I decided to continue drinking and living in just this way.

My whole life long.

In the brougham we sat bunched close together. My mother's arm round Rhea's waist; Rhea nibbling her shoulder. Rhea, holding my hand, holding it as far up her leg as she could get it. I shot a glance at my mother; she appeared radiant. 'Pierre,' she said, 'forget all about me, forgive me; I'm happy.'

I still had my fear. I told myself that, this time, I'd avoid looking.

At the restaurant my mother raised her glass and spoke: 'You see, Pierre, I'm tight. That's how it is with me every day. Tell him, Rhea.'

'Oh yes, Pierre,' Rhea said, 'every day, that's just how it is. Live it all the way up, that's what we like. But your mother doesn't like men, not an awful lot. But I do. I do the liking for the two of us combined. Your mother's wonderful.'

Her face alight, Rhea stared at my mother. Both their expressions were solemn.

My mother turned towards me. Her voice was tender. 'I am happy not to seem unhappy to you any more. I have unspeakable appetites and I can't say how happy I am to tell you about them.'

Her gaze was no longer vague.

'I know what I want.' She said it maliciously. But no sooner was it born than the smile died upon those full lips which were quivering as if she were short of breath. 'I know what I want,' she repeated.

'Mother,' I said, distraught, 'I want to know what you want. I want to know and I want to love what you want.'

Rhea was considering us, she was watching my mother. But amidst all those noisy tables we were alone, my mother and I, as isolated as in a desert solitude.

'What I want?' my mother said. 'Even if it kills me, to yield to my desires, to every last one of them.'

'To the most insane, Mother?'

'Yes, my son, to the most insane.'

She smiled, or rather, laughter twisted her mouth. As though in the act of laughing she were going to eat me.

'Pierre,' Rhea said, 'I know I've had too much to drink, but your mother . . . really, she's daft, it scares me to look at her. I shouldn't tell you so, but I'm afraid. You should think about that. I've had too much to drink, but what is going to happen? You know, Pierre, I'm in love with your mother. But you are destroying her, Pierre. You are keeping her from laughing and your mother has got to laugh in order to live.'

'Why,' I said to Rhea, 'my mother is looking at me and she is laughing this very minute. What can I do, Mother? I'd like . . . We've had too much to drink.'

'Rhea has drunk too much, you have drunk too much. Pierre, think of those days when you would be asleep, and I would hold my hand on your forehead. You would be shaking from fever; my misfortune is that in my excesses I never find the trembling happiness I got from you. Pierre, Rhea hasn't understood me and you may perhaps not be willing to hear. But you saw me laugh; when I was laughing, I was thinking back to the moment when I thought you were going to die. Pierre? Oh, I'm going to cry, I don't care if I do. Don't ask me why, don't ask me anything.'

Clearly, she would have broken into sobs, had she not controlled herself with a tremendous effort.

'Rhea,' she said, 'you were right. Now for God's sake make me laugh!'

Rhea leaned close to me, spoke in my ear. Her proposition was obscene, and my answer, arising out of the confusion of reactions that had us all three on the verge of something lunatic, was an irrepressible loud laugh.

'Tell me,' my mother said to me.

'Lean near,' Rhea said to her, 'I'll tell you.'

My mother leaned close to Rhea. Gales of infantile laughter from us all; Rhea's obscene proposition was so absurd, so unseemly, that our insides knotted, hurt, there in the middle of the crowded room. Already hilarious, we were getting stares from the other diners who, not knowing what was going on, were gazing at us stupidly.

Open-mouthed, some of them were hesitating, whilst we, too far gone to stop, only laughed the harder because of the hesitation we sensed around us: then the entire restaurant started laughing, but of course without knowing why, which made things worse; things reached a point where the situation was not funny but painful and infuriating. All that undue laughter died out after a while, but in the ensuing silence one girl, having held herself in check up until now, let go all by herself— which set the whole room off again. At length, heads bent furtively over their plates, that roomful of people emerged from the spell; nobody dared look at anyone any more.

But I alone, helpless and wretched, was still going on. Rhea addressed me in a whisper: 'Think about me, think of yourself with your back to the wall and think about me.'

'Yes,' my mother said, 'your back against the wall.'

'I shall have you that way,' said Rhea, her face expressionless.

Reiterating her proposition, she now framed it in terms which barred me from laughing, terms which could only exasperate my desire.

'I am your bitch,' she added, 'I am dirty, I am in heat. If we were not in this room but somewhere else, you'd see, I'd be in your arms in a flash, naked.'

Sitting opposite us, as she refilled our glasses, my mother said, 'I give you to Rhea, I give her to you.'

I drank. Our heads were beginning to reel.

'I'm going to misbehave,' Rhea said. 'Put your hand underneath the table. Here. Look.'

I looked at Rhea: there, underneath the table, nothing but her hand was hiding what she was doing.

My glass had been filled; I emptied it.

Rhea said to me, 'If we were somewhere in the woods, Pierre, I'd have my legs in the air right now.'

I told her to stop.

'I'm out of my mind,' Rhea said.

'I want some more to drink. I can't drink any more, I haven't the strength. Take me away from here.'

Tears welled slowly from my eyes.

'Look what has happened, Rhea,' my mother said, 'we have gone perfectly mad. We've drunk too much, and now we're drunk, all three of us. It was too perfect. Be good now, Pierre, stop crying. We are going to go home.'

'Yes, Mother, let's go home, and no more. It's too wonderful, it's too awful.'

It was then that we began to sense the chill and the fear in the stares that had been trained upon us.

I noted that my mother was very calm, very sure of herself. What this implied had not yet dawned upon me by the time I got into the brougham; and there I fell asleep. Rhea and my mother knew that their delirium would survive this little interruption . . .

But, docile (I was limp, I was half unconscious), I let them put me to bed.

At lunch the next day my mother spoke to me.

She was wearing black but, though I was struck by her self-control, she gave me an impression of extreme but contained excitement. As usual, she was waiting for me in the drawing-room, sitting on the sofa. Sitting down beside her, I kissed her, I clasped her in my arms. I was near to queasiness. I was trembling.

We sat still awhile. Finally I broke the silence.

'I am happy,' I told her, 'but my happiness cannot last, I know it.'

'About yesterday?' she asked. 'Are you happy about yesterday?'

'Yes, I adore you when you are that way; but — '

'But what?'

'Everything is going to be turned upside-down.'

'Of course.'

She hugged me tighter. It was soothing and very good. But I said to her, 'I don't need to tell you: we have held each other tight, but the happiness it gives me hurts like a poison.'

'I think we are expected at table,' my mother said.

We took our places there and the orderly arrangement of things in the dining-room, the carefully set table, brought me relief. The ice-bucket contained a bottle, but only one.

'Are you beginning to see?' my mother went on. 'Pleasure only starts once the worm has got into the fruit, to become delightful happiness must be tainted with poison. All the rest is childishness. I'm pushing you, yes, and I am sorry. You would have had plenty of time to find that out for yourself. There is nothing more touching, more appealing than childishness. You were such a little boy, though, and I am so corrupted that I was forced to choose: either write you off or else talk to you . . . I believed that you had the stuff in you to cope with me. You have an uncommon amount of intelligence, but it obliges you to recognize what your mother is; you understand, and you have good cause to be appalled. Had you not been intelligent I'd have concealed myself as though from shame. But I am not ashamed of myself. Quick, open the bottle. Looked at coolly, our situation is altogether bearable — and you're no more a coward than I am. For that matter, cold lucidity is more advisable in such a situation than blind passion. But with wine's warmth in us we are better able to understand why the worst is preferable . . .'

We picked up our glasses and I gazed at the clock.

'The hand doesn't for one instant stop moving,' I said to my mother. 'A great, great pity.'

I knew, we both knew, that in the state of ambiguity in which we were living, everything tended to disintegrate swiftly, to trickle away between the fingers.

My mother called for more champagne.

'Just one bottle,' she said to me.

'Yes, one bottle, perhaps. And yet . . .'

Lunch ended, upon the sofa we were again entwined in each other's arms.

'I drink to your amours with Rhea,' my mother said to me.

'But I am afraid of Rhea,' I replied.

'Without her,' were the words that came back, 'we would be done for. It's owing to her that I can be a little reasonable: she is so mad. You too, today, will discover the good that can be got from her. It's two o'clock now; I shall be home by seven. We'll all three go out for dinner, afterwards you and she will spend the night together.'

'You are going to leave?'

'I am going to leave. I know: you'd like to bring time to a halt. Well? Well, you arouse me. And it's not in my power to make you happy. If I stayed I'd take pleasure from making you unhappy. I want you to know me thoroughly. I bring unhappiness to everyone who loves me. That's why I seek my pleasure from women whom I can use without caring. I don't mind causing suffering, but it's an exhausting pleasure. For you . . .'

'Mother, you know that you make me suffer.'

She laughed, but that equivocal laugh resembled the one she had laughed the night before, in the restaurant, when she

had been talking to me about death, and at the same time had
been on the edge of tears.

'I am leaving,' she said.

But she pressed kisses on my cheeks, buried me beneath
kisses.

'Quick, go on. Till it kills,' she added. 'You know your
mother is cracked.'

Quickly I thought of the sole remedy for my suffering. To
heighten it; to yield to it.

I filled my lungs with Rhea, drank her breath. I focused my
thoughts upon the obscenity, upon the pleasures I saw Rhea
drowning in. I recalled the photographs, I understood more of
their significance. Into my ear Rhea had slipped words which
were throttling me, burning in my veins, and, this time,
producing an ever more painful cramp in my loins. Rhea had
guided me, had steered my hand towards penetrable wetness,
and when she had kissed me she had thrust an enormous
tongue into my mouth. Rhea, whose eyes I had seen shining,
Rhea, whom I could still hear laughing from sweet
drunkenness and from the unavowable pleasure my mother
had given her. As imagined by me, that glorious creature's
existence was defined in the fornication — stark, breathless,
insatiable — of the girls shown in the pictures. But Rhea was
the most beautiful of all, and for me exemplified that ceasless
carnival of love-making into which I had decided to plunge
and never emerge. Dotingly, I repeated to myself 'Rhea's
behind', that being the part — but more vulgarly designated
by her — which she had offered to my young virility. This part
of Rhea which I longed to see with my eyes, and which, upon
her invitation, I meant to abuse, it was taking shape in my
mind: before me I beheld the shrine of mad laughter,
simultaneously emblematic of, or redolent with the funereal
aspects of, the flush toilet. I laughed, but it was a mirthless
laugh: it was mad laughter all right, but it was toneless, it was

morose, sly, it was hapless laughter. The idea of the part of
herself Rhea had proposed to me, its location and the comic
stink which everlastingly tokens our shame gave me the
feeling of being happy, of a happiness more precious than any
other, of that shameful happiness nobody else would have
coveted. But Rhea, the shameless Rhea, she would be tickled
to death to provide it, just as I ferociously craved to taste it. I
blessed her for the ludicrous gift she would make me when,
rather than my mother's pure brow, to me she would present
what it was craziness to present to my kiss. From within my
fever, pitched to its extreme, I murmured, 'From you I want
the unutterable pleasure you offer, *calling it by its name.*'

And I borrowed the words that had come from Rhea's
mouth, I articulated them, and I savoured their turpitude.

I realized once I had pronounced those words — my face
was aflame — that Rhea proposed the same thing to my
mother; I realized at the same time that my mother did
likewise. All that my train of thought gave rise to acted like a
hand at my throat, but strangling increased my pleasure. I
had the twofold feeling of laughing my head off and of being in
death's throes, and from the spasm that was shaking me,
which was bringing me joy, I felt I was going to die. And just
as I had given real utterance to Rhea's obscene proposition, so
it was that, in my prostration, I asked aloud for death. Well
did I know that, alive, I would be the dog returning to this
vomit in no time. For the most unspeakable aspects of our
pleasures are the ones we are most tightly fettered to. That is
why, like a fool, I was able to decide to ask for confession, to
back out of the pact I had only just concluded with my
mother. The idea of God is pale next to that of perdition, but of
this I could have no inkling in advance. The unnameable
caress which had been proposed to me (and which, I
supposed, my mother relished), it alone justified my
trembling. This caress alone was tragic: it had the suspect
savour and the glaring awfulness of lightning. I knew that my
confession would be insincere and that nothing henceforth

would shield me from the desire I had now, had had the night before, for ignominy. About that savour and about death I now knew what I had not the courage to tell myself: that my preference was for death, that I belonged to death, that in owning a desire for the hideous, the ludicrous caress, I was beckoning to death.

All the way to the church, where in my distraction I had resolved to go up to the first person I found, I was prey to uncertainty. I did not even know whether I wasn't going to turn around without waiting and go home, and, as soon as my mother returned, talk to her about seeing Rhea again. Within me everything teetered. The fall was near, did not everything tell me so? And from fear of irritating my mother, my strongest wish was to hasten it. I hurried into the confessional, eager to recite my sins, knowing full well that I'd be that much sooner able to forget, to turn my back upon this remorse I would tell the priest I had but which in truth I did not have. When the moment came to accuse myself of everything my mother was accomplice to, I balked, stopped. I thought of walking out, and stayed and finished instead, but that was from mere cowardice in which defiance of sacrilege combined with a refusal to betray my mother. Throughout I was in the grip of temptation, I revelled in it; stricken by it, I dwelt in rapturous anguish upon Rhea's nakedness. Not for an instant did the thought of God influence me; rather, if I sought Him it was in delirium, and in the delight of temptation. I was seeking nothing but the terror of evil, I wanted nothing but to have the feeling of destroying my capacity for inward peace. I felt absolved from the suspicion I had nourished of having asked for quarter, for calm, of having been afraid. Had I uttered anything about my mother's unutterable role? I was, I was thrilled to be, in a state of mortal sin. In a little while I was to see my mother again, and my heart leapt in my breast, overflowing with joy. I thought of the shame my mother was fondly at home in; thinking of it brought me distress — an overpowering, perhaps insane distress — but, I now knew, from distress my delight was going to flower. No trace of ambiguity entered into the respect I had for her. And yet, at the idea of her loving kisses I choked with this delight that distress created. What doubt could I now have of my mother's sweet complicity? I was at the height of a happiness that made me tremble, I enjoyed it all the more intensely for trembling. My mother, I reminded myself, had preceded me into vice. Vice is a treasure, of all treasures the most desirable and the most inaccessible. Like a potent drink, these thoughts fermented, boiled in my mind, and an excess of happiness raved within me. I had the feeling the whole earth was mine. There is no limit to my happiness, I cried. And how else would I have been happy if I had not resembled my mother, if I had not been, like her, certain of getting drunk on wickedness.

Now that it was resolute, my desire was already intoxicating me; I don't think that drinking could have got me more drunk than I was on my happiness. I walked into the house laughing. At that my mother raised her eyebrows, especially when I told her I had just come from church. I concluded, 'You know what Rhea proposed to me. And I'm laughing, Mother; I reached a decision in my prayers, I decided to take up Rhea's proposition.'

'Pierre, I don't believe I have ever known you to be rude before. Come, kiss me, hug me in your arms.'

'Ah, Mother, what complicity — '

'Yes indeed, my Pierre, what complicity. Let's drink to it.'

'Mother,' I stammered, 'Mother.'

I folded her in my arms.

'Champagne's ready,' she said. 'I don't remember having felt so gay in ages. Let's prepare things. Drink up, son of mine. The carriage has gone to fetch Rhea; when I hear it drive in — but that won't be for a while, I have time to drink with you — when I hear it I'll go put on my prettiest dress. Blush! Then we'll go have dinner in a quiet place I know. I want to have fun with you, laugh with you as if I were your age. But after dinner I'll say good-bye. You'll be alone.'

'I worship you, Mother. But I can't help . . . '

'You can't help?'

'I will be sad if you leave . . . '

'Oh, but I'm so much older than you, Pierre, one has only to look at me . . . Why, when I was your age I used to tear my clothes in the briars, I lived in the woods.'

I glanced at her, then poured the champagne.

'I'd like to live with you in the woods.'

She took the glass I handed her. 'No, Pierre, I used to run about the woods alone. I was crazy. And it's true, I'm crazy in the same way today. But in the woods I rode on horseback, I'd take off the saddle and I would take off my clothes. Listen to me, Pierre; I used to gallop the horse through the woods. It was when I slept with your father, I wasn't even your age: I was thirteen, and I was wild. Your father came upon me in the wild. I was naked, my horse and I, I thought we were two animals of the wild.'

'That was when I was conceived.'

'It was when you were conceived. But as far as I am concerned your good-for-nothing father had no part, or practically no part, in the story. I preferred being alone, I was alone in the woods, I was naked in the woods, I was naked, I rode horseback, naked to the skin. I was in a state . . . I shall die without ever recapturing the state I was in. I had forebodings, dreamt of girls or of fauns; I knew they would have got in my way. Your father got in my way. But when by myself I would twist on the horse, writhe, I was monstrous and — '

Tears suddenly appeared in my mother's eyes. I put my arms around her.

'My child,' she said, 'my woodland child. Hold me tight; you issued from the foliage of the forest, from the damp forest dews that gave me joy, but your father — I didn't want him, I didn't want that, I was bad-tempered. When he found me naked he raped me, but I got my nails into him, I tried to claw his eyes out. I wasn't able to.'

'Mother!' I cried.

'He'd been lying in wait, biding his time. I think he was in love with me. I was living alone with my aunts then, those old fools you may vaguely remember.'

I nodded.

'Those fools let me have my way and you were born in Switzerland. But once back from there I had to marry your father. He was your age, Pierre, twenty. I made your father horribly unhappy. From the very first day I never let him come near me. He took to drinking; he was hardly to be blamed. "Nobody," he would say to me, "nobody has any idea of the nightmare my life is. I ought to have let you scratch out my eyes." He desired me like a rutting beast and I was sixteen years old, he was twenty. I fled him, I would go into the woods. I would ride out on a horse and he never caught me again, for I was on my guard. In the woods I had always been in a state of torment, but I dreaded him. I have always found my pleasure in torment, but I became sicker every day until the day he died.'

Inwardly I was trembling like a leaf. 'I'm worried now that Rhea . . . ' I began.

'Rhea won't be getting here for a good while. She is incapable of being on time. I didn't expect I would talk to you today. Never mind. Today has been the day I have talked to you. Could I have done so earlier? And could I have listened to you talk about your father's uncouthness with me? Pierre, I am despicable, I say so without weeping for it; your father was so kind, he was so profoundly unhappy.'

'I hate him,' I said.

'But I degraded him.'

'He violated you, and I am nothing but the resulting horror. When you told me you had bloodied his face it hurt me to hear it, but I would have aided you, Mother, I would have ripped his face too.'

'Pierre, you are not his son, but the fruit of the torment that would possess me in the wild. You came from the terror I mated with when I was naked in the woods, naked like the beasts that live there; terror was my joy. That joy, Pierre, would be with me for hours on end as I lay squirming upon the leaf-mould; that ecstasy bred you. With you I shall never humble myself, but there were things you had to know; hate your father if you like, Pierre, but I am the only mother you have who can speak to you about the inhuman rage that begot you. The desire burning in me was without conceivable limit, it was monstrous; I knew it, being just a child and because I was just a child. You grew and I trembled for you, you know how I trembled.'

Overcome, I wept. I wept over the fear my mother had had for my life, I wept blindly, it didn't matter, those tears proceeded from a grief that was deep and heavy; if they drowned me it was because those tears, springing from the furthermost extremity of things, carried me to the extremity of the whole of life.

'You are crying,' my mother said, 'you don't know why, but cry, cry some more.'

'Mother,' I said to her, 'they are glad tears, I think . . . I don't know any more — '

'You don't know, there's no knowing. Let me talk. Try to listen to me. Better that I talk than begin crying too. I'd prefer that when Rhea comes you greet her holding a glass rather than a handkerchief. I haven't said anything about the life your father and I led here, in this apartment. It was very different from what you must have thought. I am not sure whether I really have a taste for women; I believe I have never loved except in the woods. I didn't love the woods, I didn't love anything. I didn't love myself; but I loved, immeasurably. I have never loved anyone but you, but what I love in you, make no mistake about it, is not you. I believe that all I love is love, and in love itself only the torment of loving, which I have never felt except in the woods or the day when death . . . Anyhow, with a pretty woman I can amuse myself painlessly — exactly, without it tormenting me; it calms me;

I don't suppose I will be telling you anything you don't already know if I say that only a wild spree gives me any appreciable pleasure. But right from the outset I had affairs with girls, without that giving your father one iota of satisfaction, and it soon occurred to me to bring the poor man in on the game: an idea like that suited my aversion for regular situations. What did the depravity actually consist in? I would invite him into my bedroom and ask him to participate. You don't quite understand? Often I'd come home with two girls: one would make love with your father, the other with me. Sometimes the girls brought men along and I used them. Sometimes even the coachman . . . Time would pass, and for me that meant procuring myself people for a new orgy that evening, and I would beat your father — that also, I would beat him in front of the others. I never tired of humiliating him, I put him in women's clothes, I dressed him up as a clown and we would have dinner. I lived like an animal and, where it was a question of your father, there was no end to my cruelty. I was becoming crazy. Pierre, you will soon find out what unsatisfied passion is: it's the treadmill, you begin with whorehouse frolics, then it's drinking and lies, then it's going down deeper and deeper, death without end.'

'Mother, don't say any more.'

'Your health, Pierre. Drink up. But above all don't forget that I am no longer free: I have signed a pact with insanity and tonight it's your turn; it's your turn to sign.'

My mother laughed. She laughed that common, sneaky laugh which disgusts me, which depresses me.

'I don't want to,' I told her. 'I'm not going to leave you. You were talking quietly to me, then without warning you became a stranger, as if what you wanted was to hurt me.'

'Ah, I'm driving you crazy!'

'I am afraid so, yes. Tell me about your life in the woods.'

'No. My life now amounts to nothing more than the filth in it. You are right, Pierre, your father did get the better of me.'

'Never!' I exclaimed. 'Look at yourself, look at me! Can't you see? I am the child of the forest festival — '

'The child of lust?' she asked.
'Of course, of course, the child of lust!'

I gazed at my mother. I folded her in my arms. She was
drifting smoothly, quietly into that laden stillness of hers,
which was the stillness desire infuses, which was the ripening
of her exasperated desire. I read that tranquil happiness in her
eyes and knew that it was not dispelling her anguish, but was
assuaging it, rendering it pleasurable. I knew that the torment
that was destroying her was great, and greater still was the
daring which prevailed over any imaginable fear. She
believed in the fragile enchantment of delight, with its
insidious power to silence deep suffering. And even now we
were both of us soaring on the wings of the playfulness that
was conveying us back to this world of pleasure where amidst
thorns and in frenzy my mother had early discovered her
divine way. At that moment my irony, the gentle stirring of
irony in me, lent me strength to confront what would formerly
overcome me and now induced this voluptuous trembling in
me, the trembling which thereafter would always make me
smile.

In this calm silence and in this happiness unintelligible to
our own selves, I gazed at my mother. Happiness at which I
doubly marvelled, for desire was leading me less towards the
frantic outburst I had practised in solitude than towards
contemplation of a perfect depravity which, like a drug, but
with cruel lucidity, unfolded for me the dizzying prospects of
infinite possibility. In other words, I was less troubled by
Rhea, who would be able to provide me palpable relief, than
by my mother, from whom I could only expect the immaterial
ecstasies of shame. Rhea held an attraction for me,
undeniably; but in her I desired not so much the facilities of
pleasure as the object connected with my mother's disorders,
and in my mother I loved the possibility of an unbridled
licentiousness with which, for me, carnal pleasure could not
keep pace nor convert into a pleasurable satisfaction. Only

when high on alcohol or in my solitary frenzy had I been able to detach my thoughts from my mother and fix them upon her girlfriend. Where my error had lain now seemed very clear to me and I made up my mind that from now on — as if I had already done so the night before, as if I had touched, had caressed her — I would view Rhea as nothing but the indirect access to what I could not get at in my mother.

I had to leave the room for a moment; when I returned Rhea was there. There was laughter, there were kisses; amidst all that I handed round glasses and filled them. Champagne dripped to the floor. Rhea turned to me at once. 'Pierre,' she complained, 'you haven't yet kissed me.'

'I'll be back,' my mother said. 'I'm going to put on a pretty dress.'

The next instant I held Rhea in my arms.

'Pierre, I made you a promise. Remember?'

I reddened.

'Your mother herself reminded me. We laughed.'

'You do embarrass me,' I said.

She stood before me, defying me, laughing at the sight of my lipstick-smeared mouth.

(Rhea laughing at my smeared lips, her image next to mine in the mirror, and related to my surprise as I looked at myself; Rhea, whose image is for me linked inseparably with the taste of lipstick, the taste which for me remains that of licence; Rhea, there in front of me, hovering on the brink of a voluntary act of nameless obscenity, haunts me to this day. Rhea still looks at me in the same way today, but today her lovely face — or her vile face, I can just as well say her vile face — is divested of the magic of overflowing champagne. If now that face looms up in my thoughts, it takes rise out of the remote reaches of time.

To be sure, the same applies to all faces whose reflections

this story conjures up. But as distinct from the others, the remembrance of Rhea is very special, being connected with someone actually glimpsed only very fleetingly, and with an obsessing backdrop against which her obscenity stands in relief. That backdrop is the nunnery into which my mother's suicide was to chase Rhea a year later. Lucky Rhea, to have found the refuge which this story leads not towards, but away from . . .

Such indeed is my wish, enjoined by pride: that woe and nothing but woe befall him who, reading this unhappy book, is fit to invoke the one blessing worthy of the name, the only one that cannot mislead him.

Rhea failed to enact the whole of that ludicrous sacrifice; at any rate from the unlimited gift she made of her body, of the intimacy and gleefulness of her joy, she chose to except the usual thoroughfare to the limited operation.)

The implicit terror in the foregoing lines permits me to gloss over the scene that my mother's absence rendered possible. If I have dwelled upon its facetious aspects, I have thereby meant to suggest the terrible stake that was involved — which Rhea's later taking of the veil revealed.

Rhea had not the power, of her own accord, to provide a glimpse of the terror inhabiting her. And did it rightly inhabit her? If so, it dwelled in her as it does in a child who frolics on the cliff's edge and who has no sense of the emptiness below until, having slipped, nothing but the bramble hooked in its clothing saves it from disaster. The child has none the less defied the abyss.

When she got up from her awkward position Rhea was laughing.

But how could I forget those insane eyes, those eyes gazing

at me from another world, out of the depths of their obscenity?

Rhea went on laughing, her laughter changed, there was tenderness in it now.

'You made me dizzy,' she was saying.

I answered her in a gasp, 'I'm dizzy too.'

'I'll call your mother,' she said.

My mother entered on tiptoe.

She did not enter the way she had gone out, but by another door, and unseen.

When I felt her hands covering my eyes, when she burst into that wild laughter which, loud and clear and irresistible, was nevertheless alien to her (like the black velvet mask she wore the night before she killed herself), and when in my ear, out of breath, she cried a weak 'Peek-a-boo!' I thought to myself that no one had ever recaptured the gay riotousness of childhood so perversely. Wearing a stunning dress, my mother was outrageously beautiful. The low-cut back bordered on indecency. Taking her in my arms, my agitation prolonged the feelings that had been ignited in me by the thoroughgoing indecency of her girlfriend. I would have been glad to die in the throes of a tumult which, today, I do not think anything else even approaches.

A glowing Rhea passed round the glasses.

Pulling me up against her shoulder, 'My virgin,' she breathed, 'my beloved, I am your wife. Let's drink with your mother to our happiness.'

My mother raised her glass. 'To your amours!' said she, suddenly adopting the vulgar tone that would freeze me.

Rhea and I replied to the toast. We were in a hurry to drink, to resume things in the state of drunkenness corresponding to the fever in our brains.

'Mother,' I suggested, 'let's start out to dinner. I've had a few already but I want to drink some more.' I turned to Rhea.

'Is there any more wonderful mother than mine, any more divine?'

She had an immense black hat which an immense ostrich plume enveloped in snowlike purity; that hat lay upon an impalpable edifice of blonde hair; her dress was pink, the hue of her skin: although tall, my mother looked tiny to me, slight, weightless, all shoulders, all heavenly glances; in those pretentious furbelows she was the wee bird on the branch, or rather the bird's thrilling little song.

'Do you know, Mother, what you lose in such finery?' I asked. 'Your gravity, Mother: all your gravity. As if you were lifting all the weight of seriousness away from the world. You're not my mother any more. You are thirteen years old. You're no longer my mother: you are my forest bird. My head is spinning, Mother. My head is already spinning a bit too fast. Isn't it better, Mother, to simply lose one's head? I've lost mine.'

'I shall leave Rhea to you now,' my mother said. 'I'm having dinner with other friends, Pierre, they are waiting for me at the same place you are going, but we shall be in another room, just as proof against such indiscretion as yours.'

'Other friends?' I stammered.

'Yes, Pierre, other girlfriends who won't leave this hat on me long, or this dress either.'

'Ah, Mother, if it were up to me — '

'But Hélène,' said Rhea, 'you can perfectly well dine with us, for Hansi is not expecting you until much later.'

'You yourself said that we were to laugh together like children, Mother. Haven't you put on a costume for fun's sake? I want to laugh with you — so as to adore you.'

'But if I stay how am I to amuse you? It isn't easy to be made to wait.'

'We'll entertain each other underneath the table,' said Rhea. 'Just for fun. And afterwards when you go we'll have a more serious sort of fun.'

'Well, why not,' my mother said. 'The fact is I am in a mood for pranks today. However, Pierre, you may take fright. Don't forget that today my hat is ready to fall off my head and that the forest beast has the ascendant in me. Never mind, though, you'll like me the way I am. What do you suppose I was in the woods? I was unbridled, unfettered. I wore no costumes for the sake of fun.'

'I am a bit afraid, I admit, but I want to be afraid. Mother, make me tremble.'

'Then drink,' she told me. 'And now look at me.'

Her eyes avoided mine. She was giggling. She had dirt on her mind and, grown sly, her attitude towards me seemed simply one of hatred; her lower lip had tucked under her front teeth.

'Come along,' Rhea cried, 'let's make him laugh. Pierre, it's time to behave idiotically — we mustn't stop drinking, though. Hélène is going to laugh, too. Your turn, Hélène, when you're ready. Pierre looks as solemn as a judge.'

'He's such a ninny,' my mother declared. 'We'll make him laugh.'

'It's so nice being silly,' I said to them, 'when one is amidst wantons. Ah, go right ahead! Make me laugh. And let me pour you something to drink.'

Rhea covered me with lipstick again, and, fondling me, excited me so insidiously that I quivered like one of the damned.

'The carriage is there,' said my mother, 'so let's be off.'

The great disorder began in the brougham. Gales of laughter. Rhea went quite berserk. When we arrived she was without her skirt, down to a pair of ample bloomers: in these she jumped from the carriage and raced up the stairs. My mother ran after her, Rhea's skirt folded over her arm. And I brought up the rear, running too, my mother's absurd hat clutched in my hand.

We dashed upstairs, we were laughing.

A waiter stepped aside, bowed, opened the door which, immediately we were all inside, my mother slammed shut with a bang.

Breathless, she flung herself upon Rhea. Then suddenly she stopped, stood up, addressed me. 'I mustn't go on, I've had too much to drink, Pierre,' she said, 'but isn't Rhea funny in her underthings, isn't she pretty! I'm positive of it, Pierre, this is the first time you've had dinner with a girl wearing nothing but her bloomers! I've become a kill-joy, I feel dreadful about it. We cannot go on with this mad behaviour — and my head's aching now anyhow. And so I am going to bid you good night.'

'No, Mother, you are dining with us.'

Overwrought, grey from excitement, I gazed unsmilingly at my mother and took her hands in mine. I was in the last stages of delirium. Discreetly, underneath the table, Rhea was caressing me. My mother was looking at me too, and looking daggers.

In a low murmur, almost inaudibly, I said that I would like never to have to budge.

My mother looked at me for a long moment. Rhea nestled herself cosily between us on the sofa, Her bloomers gaping in front and her left hand buried beneath the flesh-coloured dress.

'Those glasses on the table over there, there is nothing in them. Too bad, isn't it?' my mother observed.

'I'll get the bottle,' Rhea said.

She rose, but her buttons were undone, the bloomers slid down. My mother smiled, sucking on her lower lip.

I took the bottle from her hand. Her behind bare, she sat back down again and her hands went back to their discreet occupation.

After a little while Rhea said in a subdued voice, 'Hélène,

I'm not yet in private dining-room attire. You ought to take off my corset — for I can't do it myself, being busy, as you see.'

The black lace corset Rhea had on went no lower than her waist; it supported her breasts, it also supported her stockings.

If we were alone, she and I, I'd not be able to stand it, I was thinking. I'd be afraid of Rhea, I'd bolt.

'I haven't the courage to leave you two,' my mother groaned.

'Let's eat now,' said Rhea, removing her hands from where they had been, 'but first let's have a sip to drink.'

My mother on one side, I on the other, we leaned together over Rhea who drank between us. Up until this point our silence had only intensified our pleasure, revealed in the darkening of our faces. For several minutes my mother and I used Rhea, doing to her, and just as deliberately, just as slyly, what a few moments before she had been doing to us. We ate; once again my mother's aroused gaze and mine met and they coupled. At length we had to interrupt our game.

'Champagne, Pierre, give me some champagne,' Rhea begged. 'I'm not hungry any more. You two have just wrecked my nerves. I want to drink and I'm going to keep at it until I'm under the table. Pour me some champagne, Pierrot my love, I want a full glass, mine, thine, drink and don't stop, and not to your health any more, I drink to my caprice, you know what I count on from you. You are going to find out that as regards pleasure, I'm crazy about it. Crazy, do you hear, I love pleasure, but I love it in a way that scares me, and in no other way. Your mother — '

'She has gone,' I told her. My throat was dry.

'Gone? Did you hear her go? She wasn't in our way, was she? I'd have liked knowing she was here; but she didn't want to be. Queer, isn't it, to be afraid? But if it didn't frighten us it would bore the shit out of us.'

'Oh!' she said. She wasn't joking.

The word had jarred me as it had her. I reached for her and kissed her with a sort of grinning nastiness.

'I'd forgotten about her,' I told Rhea. 'You being naked.'

'Naked,' she repeated. 'You're having your first girl, but I'm the filthiest-minded one you could have got hold of.'

My tongue played in her mouth. I gazed at Rhea as I had gazed at my mother.

'Rhea,' I said to her, 'I don't know whether I have a filthy mind, but of one thing I am sure, I am atrocious.'

I had made love with Rhea; or rather, and more truthfully, I had spent my fury upon her. My mother had left me, I would have liked to cry, and those shudderings while we were embracing were the aching sobs that racked my heart.

The thunderbolt blazing in the sky is the brightness of death itself. My mind raves in the sky. Never does the mind rave so well as in its dying.

Not once in my violent passion for my mother did I imagine that she might become my mistress, even at such times as she let go completely. What would this love have meant if I had lost one iota of the immeasurable respect I had for her — and which, it is true, was my despair? There were moments when I wanted to be beaten by her. This desire horrified me, yet sometimes I ached from it; in it I saw my crookedness, my cowardice. Between her and me there could never by anything. Had my mother chosen to hurt me, I would have cherished the pain she inflicted upon me, but I would not have been able to grovel before her: to grovel, would that have been to respect her? To enjoy that adorable pain, I would have had to strike her in return.

I remember how one day Hansi repeated to me a remark my mother had made to her (Hansi, the only one of the girls with whom I was able to live for any length of time — in happiness, sleek happiness). Hansi: my mother had sought to corrupt her, and had failed. When we separated she married a remarkable person — I was acquainted with him — who gave her a happy, well-balanced life; by him she had a child, and it was a joy each time I saw that child. After we had broken off she continued to sleep with me, but it was not often; she still loved me, but not in the same way as before, she would have liked to cure me, and she was indeed soothing, always restoring me to the still night-time of an untroubled and yet unbounded sensuality. My mother had said to her that it was not wrong to do what she asked of her, but to wish to survive it: her idea was to involve Hansi in an orgy so thoroughgoing that death alone could terminate it. Although familiar enough with my mother's extravagant character, in this notion of hers Hansi saw cold irony and nothing more. Not that she was unconscious — far from it — of the dangerous implications of pleasure carried to the extreme, but she thought that for my mother — as for herself — there was no such thing as a guilty pleasure; and so she interpreted this as a statement on my mother's part of the impossibility of fulfilling the desire which, if incompatible with reason, leads to death. True, Hansi's cruelty — and she was capable of unbelievable cruelty — lent appreciable support to her thinking. However, my mother had probably spoken without any irony at all. Hansi is very subtle and exceedingly intelligent. Even so, she cannot fully have grasped what lay behind the apparent serenity or, to borrow the expression she herself used, the 'depraved majesty' of my mother. Vaguely, though, she did grasp it: my mother frightened her, my mother for whom Hansi had been very important. More important than any other except Charlotte, who was my cousin but whom, however, I was not to come to know until long afterwards. But Charlotte, like my mother, belonged to that species for whom sensual pleasure and death have the same dignity — and the same indignity — the same violence and nevertheless the same sweetness.

What is most obscure in my affair with my mother is the ambiguity it derived from a small number of risqué episodes, episodes in keeping with the libertinage which encompassed my mother's life and gradually came to rule the whole of mine. At least twice we had let a shared delirium link us more

profoundly and in a more indefensible manner than actual
love-making could have done. Of what we were about we had
both been aware, and even while in the midst of the cruel effort
we agreed had to be made in order to avert the worst, we
laughingly admitted to employing the roundabout means
which enabled us to go farther, and to attain the inaccessible.
But we would not have been able to endure doing what lovers
do. Never did satisfaction release us from each other as does
the blissfulness of sleep. Just as Tristan and Isolde had
between them the sword for ending their love when it became
sensual, so Rhea's naked body and nimble hands until the end
remained evidence of a dreading reciprocal respect which,
keeping us apart even at the height of our frenzies, kept the
sign of the impossible upon the passion that was devouring us.
I could defer telling how it all ended: the day my mother
realized that in the long run she must yield, and release in the
sweat of the sheets the tension that had propelled me towards
her, and her towards me, she hesitated no longer, and killed
herself. Am I then to say of this love that it was incestuous?
The insane sensuality we hovered in, was it not impersonal
and similar to that so very violent sensuality which my mother
had experienced when she wandered naked in the forest,
where my father had raped her? The desire that often knotted
in me when I was with my mother, it made no difference to me
if I satisfied it in someone else's arms. Easily, frequently, we
would, my mother and I, find ourselves in the state of the
woman or the man who desires, and in this state we would
rage, but I did not desire my mother, she did not desire me.
She would be as I knew she used to be in the wild, I would hold
her hands and know that in front of me she had turned into a
maenad, that she was in the most literal sense deranged, and I
would share her frenzy. Had we translated our trembling
madness into the barren acts of copulation, the cruel game we
played with our eyes would have ceased: I would have ceased
seeing my mother ecstatic at the sight of me, my mother would
no longer have seen me beholding her in ecstasy. We'd have

exchanged the purity of the unattainable for a mess of pottage,
to satisfy our immediate greed.

Was I even in love with my mother? I *worshipped* my mother, I
did not love her. As for her, I was the forest child, creature of
ungodly joy; she had cherished this creature with a childlike
devotion, the steadier counterpart of that extravagant
tenderness, anxious and gay, which she would lavish upon
me, not often but with dazzling effect. I sprang from the magic
of her childhood games, and it is my belief that she never came
to love any man, and did not ever love *me* in the sense that
Hansi loved me, but in all her life had just one great desire —
to captivate me and then destroy me in the scandal she had
chosen for her own destruction: no sooner had she opened my
eyes than she began to mock me, her temper rose, her
affections changed into an unabating urge to corrupt
me, into caring for nothing in me but the corruption I was
foundering in. But in all likelihood she thought that
corruption, being the best in herself, was at once the path to a
splendour whither she was leading me, and the fulfilment in
which that childbirth she had wanted must conclude. It was
still the fruit of her womb she loved, nothing was more foreign
to her than to see in me a man she might love. A man never
occupied her thoughts, never penetrated her except to slake
her thirst there in the desert where she burned, where her wish
seemed to be that, along with her, the silent beauty of
anonymous and undifferentiated persons undergo foul
destruction. In this kingdom of lust there was no room for
tenderness: the gentle and loving were banned from this place
to which the Gospel bade the violent go with their rapine. My
mother destined me for that violence over which she reigned.
There was in her and for me a love like the one that, so mystics
tell, God reserves for His creature, a love appealing to
violence, excluding peace from the heart for ever.

That passion was diametrically opposed to the love I had for Hansi, and Hansi for me. I had known it for a long time before my mother drove us out of our kingdom of tenderness. Hansi: I would tremble from fear of losing her, I sought her as the thirst-stricken seek the fountainhead. Hansi was the only one: had there been no more Hansi, no one else could have consoled me. When my mother returned from Egypt that homecoming did not gladden me: I thought, and I was right to think, that my mother would immediately destroy my happiness. I am able to tell myself that I killed my father; it could be that my mother died from having yielded to the tenderness of the kiss I laid upon her lips. Even as I bestowed it, that kiss revolted me, and I am still grinding my teeth over it. The death my mother chose that same day to die seemed to me so directly the result of it that I did not cry (but tearless pain is perhaps the worst). I hardly dare say what I think: that the love which bound us, my mother and me, belonged to another world. When I die I want it to be under torture (at least that is what I say to myself); obviously, I'd not be strong enough, all the same I'd like to laugh when I go to my death. I have no desire to behold my mother again, no, not even by some insidious means to resurrect her elusive image, the image that wrings out of me a sudden groan. The place my book allots her, that is the place she still has in my mind. Most often it seems to me that I worship my mother. Could I have stopped worshipping her? Yes: what I worship is God. Yet I do not believe in God. And hence am I mad? One thing only I know: if I were to laugh while being done to death, however fallacious the idea may be, if I were to laugh I would be responding to the question I posed as I gazed at my mother, that my mother posed in gazing at me. Undeniably, my ideas are of another world (or of the end of the world: sometimes I think that death is the only possible outcome of the filthy debauch, especially of the filthiest, that the aggregate of human lives adds up to; and it is true indeed that, slowly, bit

by bit, our vast universe is in the process of granting my
prayer).

When the housemaid called me to table for lunch she advised
me that Madame had left Paris that same morning. She
handed me a letter from my mother.

I had woken up feeling generally wrong.

With my nerves upset, nausea established itself in my very
mind. I felt the harshness of that letter through my distress.

We have gone rather far (my mother wrote), so far that,
speaking to you now, I cannot speak to you as a mother any
more. Nevertheless I have to speak to you as if nothing
could create a distance between us, as if you could hear no
matter what I had to tell you. You are still very young, still
too close to the time when you used to pray . . . I cannot
help that. I am myself furious over what I have done. But
I'm used to such situations and can't pretend to be
surprised at the lengths my madness carries me to. I dare
say you appreciate the courage it requires for me to address
you the way I am doing, as though we had, as though we
could not fail to have the strength to persevere. Behind
these lines of mine, sorry as they are, you will perhaps
discern an effort to touch in you what they would touch if in
some inconceivable world we were bound in a pure
friendship into which nothing but our excesses entered.
Mere cant, I know. And it is distasteful to me. But my
helplessness and my distaste do not change what I am.

For a long time, for months, possibly for years, I am
going to go without seeing you. This I feel permits me in
this letter, and separated from you as I already am by the
immense journey I have undertaken, to say to you what
would not be tolerable were we talking face to face. I am to
the core the person of whom you have gathered your
impressions. Once I have said what I have to say it will be
death for me not to be in your eyes, in front of you, what I

like being. I love the pleasures you have witnessed. They count for me, and to the point where you would no longer count for me if I did not know that you are as desperately in love with them as I. But 'love', the word is not enough to convey it. I would stifle if for a single instant my life ceased to illustrate the truth which inhabits me. Pleasure is the whole of my life. I have done no choosing and I know that without the pleasure in me I am nothing, that everything for which my life is waiting would not exist. It would be the universe without light, the stem without the flower, existence without life. Such talk is pretentious, but, more than that, it is insipid next to the turmoil which has me in its grip, which blinds me to such an extent that, lost in the midst of it, I see nothing, I know nothing else any more. Writing to you, I am made to realize how impotent words are, but I know that in the long run, despite their impotence, they will get through to you. When they do you will have an intimation of what is maddening me, driving me stark mad. What madmen say about God pales beside the cry this shattering truth wrests from me.

Everything that holds together in the world now keeps us apart. We could never meet again without disturbing one another, without disorder, this must not happen again. What binds you to me, and me to you, now binds us to the intolerable, and will go on doing so, and we are separated by the profoundness of that bond. What is left for me to do? Offend you, destroy you? Yes; but it does not suit me to resign myself to silence. I may hurt you; but speak to you I shall. For it was from my heart I brought you forth and if one day my heart was lifted it was from having told you about the rapture I conceived you in; but my heart, and you yourself — how can I distinguish them from my pleasure? From my pleasure, from your pleasure, from what, in the way she was able to, Rhea gave the two of us? I speak about it; it happened, and because it did it ought, I know, to compel me to silence. But I speak of my heart, of that child's

heart whence I brought you forth, whence comes and shall
ever come this blood-tie which decrees that in my suffering
I must moan close beside you, that in yours you must moan
at my side; there is more to it than suffering and sounds of
suffering, I speak also of the surpassing joy which overbore
us when, hand in hand, we would look at each other. For
our agony was the pleasure that swept us away — which,
thanks to Rhea, was a low pleasure, thanks to her as low as
it needed to be. Rhea did not really caress me; under her
touch I writhed and in front of you raved inwardly as —
before there was any you — I writhed and inwardly raved
conceiving you. It is too late for me to stop speaking; what
suffers in me, what still cries madness in me forces me to
speak. I would not have been able to set eyes on you again.
What we did cannot be redone and yet, were we together, I
would think of nothing but doing it again. And, writing to
you, I know that I cannot speak to you, but there is no way
of preventing myself from speaking. I am going abroad, as
far away as possible, but everywhere I go I shall be in the
same delirium, the same whether far from you or near, for
the pleasure in me depends on no one, it emanates from me
alone, from the imbalance in me which perpetually frays
my nerves. You can see it for yourself, you aren't the cause
of it, I can do without you and I want you at a distance from
me, but if you are involved, if it be a question of you, then I
want to be in this delirium, I want you to behold it, I want it
to destroy you. Writing to you, this delirium has beset me;
my whole being shrinks, my suffering shrieks inside me, it
tears me loose from myself in the same way I succeeded,
when I bore you, in snatching you out from inside me. In
this contorting, in this unseemliness, I resolve into a cry,
not of love, rather of hate. I am twisted by anguish and by
delight as well. But it is not love's delight, the only thing
possessing me is rage. My rage brought you into the world,
this rage which should be silenced but whose strident
sound, I realized yesterday as I was looking at you, that you

were hearing. I do not love you, I remain alone, but you hear this lost cry, you will hear it incessantly, it will go on scalding you incessantly, and I, until death takes me, I shall go on living in the same state. I shall live in the expectation of that other world where I will be in ecstasies of pleasure. I belong body and soul to that other world and so do you. I have absolutely no interest in this world where they scratch about, patiently waiting for death to enlighten them. As for me, it is the wind of death that sustains the life in me, I would cease to exist for you if for one instant you forgot that, for me, it is the breath of pleasure. By pleasure I mean equivocal pleasure. I have told you about the forest and about the outrages against propriety I went there to seek. Nothing was so pure, nothing so holy, nothing more violent than my forest joy. But there was a preamble to it, but for which there would not have been any pleasure and in the forest I would not have been able to divest myself of this world so as to find the other. What took the clothes off the little girl at the entrance to the woods was her introductory reading in the loft at Ingerville. I bequeath to you a vestige from that loft. In the drawer of the dressing table in my room you will find a volume titled *Maisons closes, pantalons ouverts*: cheap stuff, poor not just in title but throughout, but from it you will nevertheless get an idea of what for me was deliverance. If you could but know how I smelt the woods when I discovered, strewn before you, on the floor, the paternal photographs. Lying there in the same dust! I wanted to kiss your soiled face. The dust of the loft! How well I knew in what state . . . the only one I wanted for myself, the one I shall forever invoke, the one I wanted for you, the one for which, the day I was overcome by fury, having wanted it for you, I yearned, I ached: that state before which there is no one who in public does not turn away in shame. I dreamt that you might see my glazed eyes then, thirsting for your downfall and for the grief it would cause you. I am sure that never — and I would refuse . . .

But I wanted to introduce you into my realm, which is not only that of the forest but that of the loft too. I made you a gift of fever when you were in my womb and it is some more of my fever I give you by urging you farther on into the mire where we are both caught together. With you at my side I am proud to turn my back upon all the others, do you sense it? But I'd strangle you if deceitfully — or blatantly — you were to adopt the others' attitude and to decline my attic realm.

I am taking Rhea with me. To you I am leaving Hansi, whom you do not know. I was unable to corrupt Hansi, and, notwithstanding the trouble I went to, she's a mere girl — a mere girl in looks only? perhaps, but if her looks deceive it's only slightly — whom I am putting in your bed. But she knows where she is being put, and will be waiting compliantly for you tomorrow. When you cast eyes upon Hansi you will no longer doubt that smiling goddesses stood round your cradle. In the meantime, those goddesses are also the deities of my loft . . .

As I said before, when I read this I was overcome by nausea; I had no clear grasp either of the new turn my relations with my mother were taking or of where I was left by this appointment with a girl she had seduced. It seemed to me useless to hope for release from this harrassing, perhaps wonderful, discomfort. I was relieved by my mother's departure, and in the fog where I was lost I felt that this letter was the very one I had been waiting for, that it spelled dreadful unhappiness for me but that it would give me the strength to love.

The rendezvous my mother had arranged was in a place like the one where she and I had dined with Rhea. Two days before leaving me she had joined Hansi in the same house but in another room on another floor; she (or else Hansi) probably wished to forestall oppressive reminders of that previous evening. And now I waited for the scheduled meeting. It was an unbearable wait, but waiting provides respite. I spent it re-reading my mother's letter ten times over. I steeped myself in that letter, it even occurred to me that I ought to drink something in order to understand it, in order to reinforce the connection between drunkenness and the anguish-ridden world it disclosed to me. I arrived on time, entered the downstairs salon; I wouldn't have been able to shut the door or take a seat, nothing could have made me turn tail and flee, but the mirrors everywhere, the gilt and the lights overhead rattled me. The attendant showed me where the bell was, pointed to where I would find the toilets concealed within a rosewood panelled cubicle. I had the impression Hansi was there, that in those cloying, overheated surroundings she had just entered and that the old man with bushy sideburns, who had once again opened the door to the water closet, was saying to her, 'This well-appearing young man will invite you to use the facilities' — and partly hiding his mouth behind one hand — 'while he looks on. Pah. Disgusting.' My impression was of a butcher's shop in midsummer, when the smell is strong. Nothing was missing there that could have helped to upset me. I recalled what my mother had added in a postscript: 'The idea of finding an unknown young man in such a shady house frightens Hansi herself. She is more afraid than you are. Even so, curiosity is winning out in her. She dislikes prudence. But your mother's closing words to you are a request that you look upon her as you would if the room where you find her were a hall in a fairytale castle.'

Anxiety kept me standing, and my feeling of being asleep and dreaming was completed by infinite reflections of my image in the mirrors lining the walls, or in those which formed the ceiling; a feeling of dissolving in a garish nightmare. I was so absorbed by my uneasiness that I did not hear the door open. My first perception of Hansi was in the mirror: standing quite close to me, she was smiling, but it seemed to me that in spite of herself, and very slightly, she was trembling. Without turning her way — I too was trembling, and I was smiling — I said to her, 'I didn't hear you . . .'

She did not reply. She continued to smile. She was enjoying the prolonged pause during which underneath that multitude of lights everything was deprived of definition.

I was a long time studying the reflection of that dream-like face.

'Perhaps', said I, 'you are about to disappear — just as simply as you came. . .'

'Will you invite me to sit down at your table?' she asked.

I laughed, we sat down and there was another long pause while we looked at one another. We entertained ourselves by looking, she and I. Looked until it hurt.

'How on earth could I be anything but intimidated,' I stammered.

'I am,' she said, and from that moment on I lay under the spell of her voice, 'I am as shy as you. If I intimidate you, you look — thank heaven! — as though you were glad to be. I too, as you can see, I'm embarrassed, but you must also see that I am happy to be embarrassed. What are you going to think of a girl for coming to find you' — her glance moved around the room — 'here . . . without knowing you at all?

'No,' she added right away, 'don't answer! Your mother spoke to me about you. But about me you know nothing.'

I rang, the old chap with the whiskers appeared, filled our glasses and began to serve us, taking his time.

The further constraint resulting from his presence and his stiff attitude had something droll about it in this house of rare and expensive sin: we felt a bond develop, to begin with through our shared amusement, then through a complicity we did not have, which this man was supposed to lend us, which it was funny, but also very pleasant, to think he would lend us.

The man left us alone at last.

'I believe', Hansi said to me, 'that if I could only cry it would be easier for me to breathe. I'm not capable of crying, and yet tears are nearer to what the situation calls for.'

'What if we were to go out?' I suggested. 'We could walk a little.'

She shook her head. 'No, for unless I am mistaken this uneasiness is doing delightful things to you too. In coming here, I agreed to what every woman agrees to when she marries. Let me try to tell you what it was in your mother's proposition that decided me. From her account of me you know that I am not an adventuress — anyhow that I haven't the sophistication of one; no broad experience prepared me for a situation I was not afraid to place myself in. When I understood it would be equally difficult for you, I was conquered in advance, I was so happy I could have danced from joy. But don't jump to the conclusion that I am really what they call a respectable girl, if I were I'd not be made up as I am, I'd not be wearing perfume. If you liked, I could use some pretty shocking terms to express what we are up to. You won't ask me to, I am speaking this way because I know you won't and because I know you will be as considerate with me as if I were some little silly who'd been born yesterday. But . . .'

'But?'

'On condition . . . that you be as excited, and that you know me to be as excited as if I was used to pleasure. I am looking you straight in the face, but if I dared to I'd lower my eyes.'

I turned red (but my laugh belied the colour in my cheeks).

'I am overjoyed to look at you, but I am glad, too, that you made me look down.'

I was watching her, but though I had reddened and though, sitting opposite her, I was filled with the delight she was to give me for such a long time, I could not check the surge of aggressiveness gripping me within.

When a girl is about to yield, a lover no sooner realizes it than he resembles the housewife who gazes at the rabbit she is about to kill as if at a treasure.

'I am so unhappy,' I said to her, 'to have to kill you. Am I not obliged to be unhappy?'

'You are as unhappy as all that?'

'I dream of not killing you.'

'Maybe, but you are laughing.'

'I dream of being happy — in spite of everything.'

'What if I were in love with you?'

'What if this enchantment I am in were never to fade away?'

'My thought in coming here was to please you, to amuse you and amuse myself. I was excited, I still am. But I did not know I would fall in love with you. Turn around.'

She had me look at the divan surrounded by mirrors.

'I am frightened of not being all a young girl is supposed to be and of having the butcher's block — what a block it is! — in front of my eyes. And yet I desire you. I have been in this room before, or rather, in another room like it. I have done things already, and I wish I never had. I wish my memory was not so filled with images, but if I did not like making love, would I be here? Only one thing I beg of you, and that is not to touch me now. It hurts me not to feel you in my arms. However, I also want it to hurt you. I don't want to kiss you, I wouldn't even be able to. Tell me that you are suffering and that you are on fire. I want to come alive through my suffering — and to feed on yours. It doesn't matter so long as you know I am yours entirely. I was from the first, since I came here. And now this trembling of mine says I belong to you.' While speaking she was twisting her hands, laughing a little, but amidst her trembling ready to cry. The silence that followed lasted a long while, but we had stopped laughing, we were eating. An unseen observer might have discerned hatred in our glassy stares.

Again, with sadness, Hansi spoke to me; her voice still intoxicated me, whenever I heard it it was a though inside me a pale flame would suddenly dart up from hot embers.

'Why aren't I in your arms? Don't ask me that, but tell me you aren't cursing me in your heart.'

'I'm not cursing you,' I said to her, 'only look at me, you'll see I am not. You are enjoying our uneasiness, I am sure of it. You know very well, too, that you could give me no greater pleasure than this uneasiness — are we not yet closer, more intimately involved than we could be . . . on the block?'

'Ah, we are, you know it. Uneasiness surrenders me to you. Say it again: you have felt what I feel.'

'I can imagine no greater happiness.'

She had my hand in hers and her hand was writhing: I saw that an imperceptible convulsion had seized her. The smile which relaxed her face had the aftertaste of pleasure's irony.

Time passed, flowed between our hands.

'You have quieted me,' she said. 'Now you are going to let me leave. I want to go to sleep and to wake up; we shall be naked and you shall be inside me. Don't kiss me, I'd be unable to part from you.'

'Why should we part from one another?'

'Don't ask me anything any more: I want to go home and sleep. I shall sleep for twelve hours. I'll see to it that I do. When I wake up I'll know you are about to arrive; I'll have just enough time to emerge from sleep.'

Little by little vagueness invaded her eyes. As if, in her simplicity and goodness, she were about to go to sleep there in front of me.

'Would you like to sleep with me?' she asked.

I did not answer.

'It's impossible, and you know it. You are going to take me home. I shall be waiting for you tomorrow. We shall go out to lunch together. After that you won't leave me again.

Neither of us said much in the open carriage. I can still remember the horse's trot, the crack of the whip; I have not

forgotten the immense stir of the boulevards dinning in a
marvellous stillness. There was an instant when, off in a
corner, Hansi turned away and laughed, as though she were
laughing at me.

We got out. A few moments later I was standing alone on the
pavement. I felt it would do me good to walk. Hansi's
happiness had left me physically disconcerted. An ache
deepened in my groin, a positive cramp soon shortened my
stride, I moved ahead limping. I thought back to the
restaurant, to the malaise we experienced there under the
glaring lights. And to our so freely indulged-in conversation.
It seemed to me that it had had the gaucherie of an
undressing, that in a sense, though there had been no final
letting go, we had experienced the deliverance ecstasy brings.
I hailed another carriage to take me home. I was in the sorriest
plight, I was becoming laughable, but that did not prevent my
excitement from remaining at its peak. I shut my eyes tight
and submitted to its tyranny. Confused, uncertain images
paraded through my mind, but I made no attempt to identify
them, only let them pass, being in a kind of dreaming state; a
very pleasant state to be in or a very unpleasant one, I'd not
have been able to say which, and whence I finally escaped,
emptied by a monstrous excess of pollution.

I woke up late, with rings under my eyes. Not a minute to lose,
I must get to Hansi's right away. I was in such a feverish hurry
I hardly had time to repeat to myself that I was hopelessly in
love with her. On the physical plane I was still hurting, but
hurting less: my pains receding, my happiness, I assumed,
was surely coming to the fore.

In the apartment I entered, in the deep easy-chair where
the pretty housemaid had me sit down, I was obliged to wait.

Anxiety stole over me. Suddenly the truth appeared. It had plenty of time to sink in. Yesterday, I thought to myself, I could not make head or tail of Hansi. Today, it is all crystal clear: the girl I fell in love with and probably still am in love with and won't be able to stop being in love with makes a business of it . . . These fancy appointments, the pert little maid who answered the door (pretty, too pretty, she had been smiling when she said it: 'Madame regrets, but she has asked me to tell you that you may perhaps have to wait a little') . . . And the night before, when she had simply had to get away as soon as possible, what had that meant? Or the ease with which, for my purposes, my mother had got hold of her, as though of a girl whose body is to be had . . . Worst of all was the feeble excuse she had offered for refusing to give herself to me our first night together. The first thing I am going to do, I told myself, is ask her with whom she has just betrayed me. Before doing anything else I must do that.

I was so upset I thought of leaving, but I had only to think of it to appreciate the extent of my helplessness. I was not going to leave. I wiped the sweat from my forehead. I didn't know what to do. A wish to re-read my mother's letter came over me. But I couldn't even do that, there was nothing for me to do except settle deeper into the wretchedness where the most absurd, the least justified passion had just landed me. I could do nothing but dwell on the object of that passion: can I complain, I asked myself, am I in a position to complain of having been betrayed? No, not even that, for to betray me she would first have had to be mine. Nor could I accuse her of anything in particular. I lacked the barest evidence. If, as I now believed, Hansi was simply an *intriguante*, then, in no time, I'd be inextricably lost amidst her innumerable lies, lies I'd be only too eager to swallow, since the thought of losing her was already enough to petrify me. My thoughts went in all directions. For a moment the recollection of her remarks induced me to believe that if she had wanted to take me in, she'd not have said the things she did. I was distressed and, too alive in me, Hansi's image fascinated me. I remembered that in the carriage she had glanced at me furtively, the while laughing up her sleeve (she had not supposed I would notice); so beautiful had she then been that, musing upon it, I felt I would be happy to have her laugh at me forever, to have her turn me into what I had read of in a pornographic book, a slave beaten black and blue, deriving pleasure from those beatings, revelling in his slavery.

I heard the key in the lock. An out-of-breath Hansi dashed in.

'Oh,' she said, 'I've made you wait. I didn't sleep a wink — doesn't it show?'

Riding crop in hand, auburn hair under the gleaming black hat, Hansi in riding habit was not only fascinating, she was the incarnation of the fantasy-figure which had just that very instant produced stirrings in me.

As though she had guessed as much! Laughter on her lips, mischief in her eyes, she leaned over me and caught my wrists.

'You are overpowered by my outfit, are you? I like it and like wearing it, but you mustn't, you decidedly must not take it for the livery of my vices. I am voluptuous and long to show you that I am; but' — and she tapped the crop — 'I am not one for using this. You're disappointed? It does make such a nice sound . . .'

I put on a long face and the crop whistled. Her eyes sparkling merrily, she grasped the whip as resolutely as a trainer putting an animal through its paces, and moved close to me.

'At my feet!' she ordered. 'Eyes on my boots!'

Then she dropped her bravado, began to laugh and, hiking up her skirt, showed me the boots she had on and their glistening patent leather.

She simpered. 'You aren't being docile at all. What a pity!

But I might as well tell you that since I had to put them on all by myself you're not going to get the chance to kiss them, so too bad for you. Ah, Pierre, tell me what makes you sad; regrets?'

She was not so much speaking to me as to herself, brimming with liveliness. She took firm hold of the whip again, snapped the thong.

'Like to know what got me into this mood? Well, coming in, I said to myself, I'm his, he's mine. Do you want me to take everything off? You prefer that I keep my hat on? My boots too? I'd like to do nothing without it being what you want. You are asking to have the crop? You want to beat me to death? I don't have much of a taste for that. The only taste I have is for being yours and for being your plaything. You're in low spirits, I can see that, but I cannot contain myself for joy, the carriage crept along so slowly I thought I would die and, afterwards, unable to sleep, I was dying from a wish to go out into the woods. Being in love has never made me suffer, I have never been in love, but it drove me nearly crazy waiting for the moment that would separate you from me. Why did I ask you to leave me last night?'

'Yes, Hansi, why did you ask me to leave you last night?'

'I wanted to find out, Pierre. I was beside myself. I wanted to be alone. Pierre, would you know what daytime was if there was never any night? But in the night, Pierre, when I was waiting for the day, the wait became awful.'

My gloom had not lifted. I was deaf to what Hansi was seeking to express, and it made me unhappy to feel at that remove from her, unhappy not to open my arms to her.

I believe she grasped what the trouble was. For she suddenly exclaimed, 'I had forgotten, Pierre; it came to me during the night while I was unable to get to sleep that you don't know anything about me.'

'I don't want to know anything . . .'

'If I sold this body would you love me if I let it go to the highest bidder?'

I looked down and muttered my reply, 'I don't care. You know I'd love you no matter what.'

'Oh, how sad you look. You had misgivings?'

I did not raise my head.

'What do I know about you? I was afraid that last night you might have lied to me in order to get away.'

'I didn't lie to you. But any girl willing to have a supper at that place must prostitute herself — you thought that?'

'I thought that. I'd accept it, but I'd lose interest in life. I often lose interest in life.'

'You'll find it again if you love me. Kiss me.'

The black top hat fell and happiness unstrung me.

For how long I lay annihilated by delight I do not know, but I heard Hansi say, 'I do not have any vices, I loathe vices, but with the pleasure I gave him I might be the death of a man. Do you know why? It's because when pleasure has hold of me I die.'

Our mouths met again, melted in a feeling of excessive joy. The tongue's slight tremor loosened the very stays of life, sped us past the whole of life: the intensity and intimacy of a sensation opened up an abyss in which everything is lost, like the deep wound which opens up at death.

'We ought to eat,' Hansi murmured.

'We ought to eat,' I replied.

But words meant nothing to us any longer. Looking at each other, what was finally disturbing was to see how our gazes swam; as if we were returning from another world. In our stinging desire, we had not even the strength to smile.

'I want to get out of these clothes,' Hansi said. 'Come into my bedroom and I'll go and change in the bathroom, you can talk to me through the doorway.'

The same childish itch had hold of us both.

'These boots won't come off for me,' she wailed.

She had to ring for her maid. She had then to show impatience. After that she was rid of her boots in a trice.

She reappeared in a filmy lace wrap. She slid into my arms,

said, her mouth offering itself already, 'My whole body hungers to give itself to you, can't you feel it? I won't dress since after lunch we shall get into bed . . . Is that going to be all right?'

Disquiet, I understood, was to season this happiness. Without sensing any need to hide the fact from her servant, Hansi was able to give herself to me, a stranger. The sole explanation was that she was accustomed to doing so.

Hansi anticipated my unspoken questions. 'Pierre, Pierre, I'm so in love, I'm so on tenterhooks I have hardly taken time to speak to you. I misled you a while ago. I realize that now.'

I waited for the rest.

'Don't be downcast. You are not my first lover, that I did tell you. Very soon you shall be my third. But I'm going to keep you. With the two others it lasted only a night. One thing, though . . .'

'What one thing?'

'I said I had no vices, hated vice. It isn't true, not exactly. Yet in a sense it is true, at least for me. Maybe it isn't a vice. I have a very attractive maid. Or don't you think so?

'You have gone red in the face. Would that mean you are already considering being unfaithful to me? I told you I was made for pleasure. You have been wondering what I do for a living. I don't do anything, I have an income that takes care of everything, leaving me independent; but if I didn't have Lulu I'd probably give myself to anyone who happened along. I don't like being alone when night falls.'

I let out a groan.

'Last night?'

'You are all unhappy. You're jealous?'

'I wouldn't want you to have lied to me.'

'Last night I took twice the ordinary dose to go to sleep but nothing worked. Early this morning, to ease the desire I had for you I toyed with the idea of doing to myself what you'd have done if you'd been there. And I'd have done it, and I wouldn't have felt sorry afterwards. I'd have told you afterwards, you'd have forgiven me. But instead I decided to get up and go for a ride in the park and to run the crazy creature's excitement out of her. Now I have your arms, I have your lips, I am the next thing to naked. I want to raise havoc with you. If I'm not depraved I am still dreadfully naughty and I adore laughing. Right now I'm almost out of my mind from impatience. But I'm holding back until you can't stand it another instant. You couldn't have heard it because it was in a whisper, but do you know what Lulu said to me when she was taking off my boots in the bathroom? You can't imagine what marvellous fun she is.'

'You call her Lulu?'

'The name fits her, don't you agree? Some day I'd love to have you come to the woods and be there while we are having a good time together, Lulu and I; she is superb in a riding costume.'

'Lulu?'

'She's no more a housemaid than I am. She is a woman who enjoys herself in life and our games are never innocent.'

'Hansi,' I said, 'I don't know why, but I want to cry.'

Hansi did not understand that those tears, which had probably already begun to come to my eyes, were tears of happiness. I was discovering what a fool I had been and, shaken, I was overcome with wonder before the richness of the gifts life dispenses, on top of love's delights those of beauty and of sensual pleasure.

'No, Pierre, I'll never make you cry. I love you so I could weep, weep from joy. Don't ever let yourself think our love is not happy. But in another moment it is going to happen. Already I have the feeling I am naked and I want to speak freely to you, without sparing a modesty for which, with me, the time is past. When we let go, let it be entirely; in another moment I am going to ask you to take me. But you don't yet know what Lulu said to me in the bathroom.'

'Hansi, no, I don't want to know now.'

'Excuse me, Pierre, I am so crazy, so crazy about you, I don't know what I am saying. I am crazy and no one has ever got me in the state I am in now. I say silly things, but it is because desire for you is maddening me. I am a sorry creature, but I am what I am. Come, my darling, take me.'

She did not take off, rather she tore off the lace that was covering her; it was she who reached for me. She helped me undress. We found ourselves in the middle of the room, entwined on the floor.

We remained several days in bed, absorbed in that delirium, covering ourselves only when Lulu came in with things to eat and drink — wine, cold meats upon which we pounced ravenously. We drank great amounts of burgundy to revive our failing strength. We were saying one evening that it could after all be that we were caught up in a hallucination, perhaps insane; while we were talking about it Hansi decided she had to have some more to drink.

'I want to get her view on the matter,' she said.

Lulu brought us champagne. 'We're both completely mixed up,' Hansi said to her; 'we wonder what's happening to us. How many days have we been here in this bed? Do you suppose we are going to melt away?'

'You're in your fourth day,' Lulu replied, laughing. 'Indeed, Madame does give me the impression she is wearing herself out. If I dared, I'd say the same of Monsieur.'

'Anyhow, the result is I don't even know where I am any more,' said Hansi.

'The result of dreaming the time away, no doubt . . .'

'No doubt!'

Both girls broke into gales of laughter.

'We'll all drink together,' Hansi proposed. 'Pierre and I shall drink from the same glass.'

'Madame permits me to say *tu* to her?'

Another burst of laughter from Hansi.

'To both of us so long as Pierre doesn't mind.'

'Your name is Pierre?' Lulu inquired.

'I feel I am reviving again,' Hansi said.

'Pierre,' said Lulu, 'you mustn't suppose we are depraved. I have my vices. Actually, the maid is simply a little queer. Not Hansi, but everyone enjoys walking on the edge of a cliff.'

'People often certain notions about me,' Hansi said to me, 'I even like to encourage them, but I don't always live up to expectations.'

'I too feel that I am reviving,' I said.

I was unable to tell why this doubletalk, which annoyed me, also pleased me.

'Is it possible,' asked Hansi, 'that you have the strength for a little dreaming?'

'Why surely,' I said, 'I am coming back to life but only in order the better to dream.'

'I ought to leave you two to your dreaming,' said Lulu.

'As you wish,' said Hansi, 'but before you do, finish the bottle, open the other one and we'll drink our farewell glass. We are going to dream, then you'll return, for we'll have further dreams to tell you.'

Lulu drank with distinct gusto. She paid scant attention to us, none to the fact that underneath the bedcover Hansi was quietly getting the game started again, and it was not until she rose that she had anything more to say. 'Will Madame give it some thought? When the maid is in a dreamy mood, she does not always feel inclined to do her dreaming alone.'

This dialogue troubled me. I could not make out what exactly my mistress expected from her friend, or her friend from my mistress. In the meantime, Hansi had so thoroughly satisfied me, she had steeped me in pleasure to such a degree . . . all the first day's tenseness had disappeared. While I did not feel drawn to it, I was not afraid of the further step on the downhill path evoked by this talk, of which Rheas's easy lack of constraint had given me an example. Because of my mother's presence, this step had become associated with anguish, but anguish does not spoil a pleasure it is able to render more acute. Slowly, thoughtfully, I put my arms around Hansi, held her still, immobilized her burning nervousness; and I considered how far I had come since the day I had, for the first time, perceived what pleasure was opening up for me. In the vast domain into which I had crept alone and slyly I was today living without fear and without regret. The religious dread I had at the beginning, I now used, made of it a secret spur to pleasure. The intimate, the inmost life of the body is so profound: from us it draws that terrible cry beside which the fit of piety is a pale peeping stammer. Vanquished piety yields only boredom. The difficulties, the problems of the flesh, its treacheries, its failings, its terrors, the misunderstandings it engenders, the maladroitness it is the occasion of, these alone provide a basis and excuse for chastity. Genital pleasure is the wealth that age, ugliness and all the forms of poverty limit. Hardly had I received this treasure than in the anger that priests vent against it I detected the complaining of irremediable impotence (exasperated by the stings of excitement). What was left of my ardent religiosity associated itself with the ecstasy of a voluptuous life, detached itself from the immense barrenness of suffering self-denial. Very soon the countenance that pleasure never transfigured ceased to seem alive to me, dissolute amusements attracted me, and I would that day have liked to invite Lulu to stay with us. The idea of making love in front of that pretty girl appealed to me, Hansi's ambiguous attitude perplexed me. If it was to be Hansi in bed with Lulu, well and good, I'd not be the least bit jealous, all I wanted to know was what she wanted.

These thoughts could not lessen the pleasure I had in Hansi's arms; the fourth day it was the same, an onrushing river bent blindly upon running itself out in the sea. No woman has given me in such a manner the inexhaustible feeling of the happiness which flows away and which cannot flow too fast. Unstaunchable wound, hence mortal. No doubt. No matter: may it bleed for ever! . . . Under the influence of the moment, I regretted having given even a thought to a piteous Lulu who could not partake in this happiness, infinite like my love, more secret than the depths of my heart and more lucid than a murder.

I was nearing the degree of emotional violence, Hansi was reaching it with me, when with regard to Lulu I might have said, 'Strangle her,' or 'lick her tongue,' either one without, in my indifference, first separating the possible from the impossible, the desirable from the absurd. Had lightning blasted me — why, in that case I'd no longer hear this fly buzzing by my ear. Lightning inhabited me, enclosed me, and I could only gradually get to that neutral ground where, speaking to my friend, I felt once again (being by then upon that bleak shore where desire leaves life stranded) the desire to say, 'A little while ago you wanted to tell me what Lulu said, what I wasn't able to hear her say to you in the bathroom.'

For a while Hansi gazed at me uncomprehendingly. Then she seemed to emerge from a dream and said, 'Of course. I ought to have parted company with her. Anyway, I want to talk to you about her and tell you what she is for me, or perhaps was.'

She smiled at me. Once again charm passed from smile into lips' sweetness, sweetness into wanting, thence into violence . . .

Calm returned. And I said to her, 'I think I'm finished this time. I am dead.'

'We should have something to eat,' she said. 'Do you suppose it is dinner-time?'

'I didn't wind my watch . . .'

'Let me ring for Lulu.'

'Ring for Lulu . . . she's your maid, isn't she — isn't that what you said?'

'Yes, Lulu is my housemaid, but . . . you know, things just aren't so simple.'

Hansi was overcome by hilarity.

'I wanted,' she said, 'I wanted to keep you quiet, to knock the talk right out of you. I haven't the strength any more, I'm seeing double. I'll ring for Lulu.'

'Tell me about her before you do.'

'First I am going to ring for her.'

'You'll speak to me in front of her?'

'Why shouldn't I?'

'Stop a moment and think!'

'I'm too weak to think.'

'First talk to me about Lulu.'

'In the bathroom my riding crop was on the chair, I had my boots on. Lulu was looking at the toe of my boots and she said that it was a pity Madame was not in her wicked form this morning. No, Pierre, I'll call her in, I'll do my talking in front of her. Though it's harder and I am dead. Believe me, I do want to talk, I have wanted to do everything with you, I want to talk. Randiness is exhausting and exhaustion makes me randier than ever. I'm going to talk.'

Lulu was at the door.

'Come in, Lulu. I'm yawning. Tonight I'm in a cynical mood. To begin with, we're famished, we want to eat, to eat and drink. After that you're going to tell Pierre everything: that you like my riding crop, that you are not my maid, that we take the act too far. I'm falling asleep, Pierre, I'm already tired of not dreaming.'

'Dinner isn't ready but she's falling asleep. Pierre, I don't really think she could have told you anything at all.'

'If I understand it, I have taken your place, but Hansi whips you and you like it. Does she like doing it?'

'It's perfectly true,' Lulu said to me, 'you have taken my place, Pierre. In a sense. For Hansi has never been in love with me.'

'You believe she is with me?'

'Pierre, it was like some cataclysm; she became so delirious that I am blissfully happy on her account, sad though I am on mine.'

'Lulu,' I said to her, 'you are beautiful and I feel very silly occupying a place that's yours. I dream of a world where jealousy wouldn't exist. Though I believe I could be jealous of Hansi, I haven't been jealous because of you. Not for a moment have I been upset because of you, but by the thought of the other lovers to whom you must have opened the door, and I was terrified to see that she wasn't in the least bothered by my coming here, as if it was the usual thing.'

'Why, no, Hansi is almost a virgin and I had the idea she disliked men. I was mistaken, she likes love-making. She would want to make love every night. And then yesterday . . . I begged her to beat me; she could do that without wronging you. She's asleep. Tell me, would it annoy you if she beat me?'

'I don't know, I am so awfully tired, I am so tired it hurts and I don't know what to think. I don't believe it would annoy me, but you, Lulu, do you get satisfaction from being beaten by her?'

'I do, but Hansi doesn't.'

'It satisfies her halfway, not wholly, but she enjoys it. Is that it?'

'No, I am pitiable and I put up with everything — she couldn't care less. She is cruel, but cruel through unconcern, she does not even take any pleasure from knowing that I suffer, and yet she drives me to despair, she knows it. You told me I am beautiful, Pierre; I live on the edge of your life, at your feet, like some domestic animal. I have loved her since we were at boarding school together. She has always liked playing in bed. When we were children she would play with me; she was the lady of the house and I was the chambermaid. And she has remained a child to this day. We are still playing, and now I live in disguise. Hansi said to me that unquestionably you would not agree to her keeping me any longer.'

'But, Lulu, it's not acceptable for you!'

'Accept, Pierre, I will be your slave, her slave and yours.'

I stared at her. 'This worries me, Lulu. I don't know what you hope for in return from Hansi, but I am afraid that from me you can hope for nothing.'

'I don't hope for anything from Hansi. I wanted her to continue to beat me. That, I know, is over with. I don't hope for anything from you. You can invite me to drink — '

'Would I mind that? But I should imagine that for you it will soon become impossible, unless . . .'

'Unless . . .'

'If Hansi still wanted, that is, to play . . . with you.'

'You would like it. . .'

'I don't know whether I'd like it, but if she liked it I would not feel jealous.'

'It doesn't annoy you to have Hansi invite me to drink?'

'On the contrary, I think I am — how shall I say — moved by it. Not that I need that in order to be . . . moved, but — well, we'd overdone it and then you appeared, whereupon . . . I'm sure, for her part, that Hansi . . .'

'Just between ourselves, Hansi herself has a very decided leaning . . . but is unwilling to admit it. Sometimes she'll joke about it and then pretend a dislike . . . I'm delighted to share a secret with you, Pierre. I feel I'd like to kiss your hand. Oh, I don't need to be told that nothing is a greater bore than masochism. But — and I take advantage of it — I'm pretty enough, I get away with a lot thanks to my looks. A madwoman who likes other women is in any case very easy to handle. Men make sterner masters, but they are apt to be more of a nuisance. Female masochists who like women make good friends, useful in all sorts of ways . . . Anyhow, your kindness has helped me regain a little courage. With luck I won't be fired.'

'Go get some champagne, Lulu. If Hansi is still asleep we'll toast our friendship. You know that I am in love with Hansi, but you also ought to know that I desire her whenever I see the two of you together.'

Lulu brought some champagne and we left the bedroom where Hansi was sleeping and went to sit down elsewhere.

'I took off my apron,' Lulu said, 'but I'll get back into my maid's uniform for dinner, which is waiting for you now.'

I uncorked the bottle. I handed Lulu her glass.

'We love the same woman,' I said to her. 'Which makes us accomplices. Let's drink to it.'

And we did. I was in a happy mood, I was laughing; 'Lulu,' I said, 'I'm going to kiss you; however, it will be on the cheek . . . You mustn't be hurt; it's Hansi I'm hungry for.'

'But I'm not fond of men, Pierre, and what I love in you is Hansi's happiness. And for all three of us that happiness means the same thing. Wake her up, I'll bring you dinner. It's about me we have been talking, you and I, but about her I am not supposed to have told you anything except, just in passing, her aversion to the form of amusement . . . that we preferred not to talk about . . .'

I went into the bedroom to wake Hansi — and showed her the form I was in.

'Splendid,' she said, wrapping her arms around me, 'but I'm too hungry, let's have dinner first.'

Lulu served us. We ate. I spoke little, drank a lot. Hansi yawned. As we ate we fought against a feeling of gradual collapse. We both announced oncoming headaches; that was about all we had to say to one another. We ate, we drank, in the hope of dulling a pain that only became sharper. Hansi said, wincing, 'I am happy even so. My eyes feel strained, but never mind, I am seeing you.'

'My eyes hurt too, yes, and I see you, and the only way to keep from feeling absolutely terrible is to make love again.'

'I don't believe you have it in you.'

'Don't I, though?' I took hold of her hand: I can't say whether it was some weakness or Lulu's entry or both that surprised me, but instead of guiding that hand downwards I raised it to my lips and kissed it. I let go after that, I drew my lips away, I wiped my moist brow with my handkerchief.

'With you', I said to Hansi, 'suffering is a delight. But it's suffering nevertheless.'

'If Madame wishes,' Lulu said to her, 'I have my nurse's cap.'

'But we haven't any orderlies, nor even a stretcher,' Hansi replied, 'there's not much you can do about that. But pretty soon we'll ask you to aid these two weary old souls back to bed. To swoon away, that, Lulu, will be quite enough for me. I feel marvellous and I wish you the good fortune of often being as close to death's door as I am at this very minute. But feeling this marvellous isn't all that funny and maybe it would be better to see how things turn out before wishing you anything. At the present time . . . I can't eat another bite, haven't the strength to chew.'

I was pale, I made a vague gesture of helplessness. I no longer had the strength to speak.

'Behold the heights of happiness!' commented Lulu.

I screwed up my face, unable to laugh at — and unable to enjoy — Lulu's remark. I grimaced, I had a pang about the complicity we had entered into and whose horror curdled me. Nausea, happiness, they were blending indistinguishably.

Hansi dragged herself to bed and fell asleep right away.

But I was unable to sleep. In vain, overtired, lost in thought as I lay at her side, I caressed her flanks, her buttocks; for a long time meditated upon them. They continued to signify the wild excess of delight with which they still seemed wet, which remained the meaning of their beauty, which, in their indecency, was defiance of the chaste God I had once loved. While feeling my pain and while feeling Hansi's, I contrasted this joy with the opposite that had succeeded it — already become remote in the obscurity of the past — the joy in God I had known. My present grief, I assumed, ought to correspond to the curse attaching to the flesh and to that happiness which deceives us. But suffering from the reverse of disappointment, in my nausea I told myself that carnal pleasure is holy; the ecstasy which followed prayer, it may have been holy too, but it was always uncertain; I used to have to force myself, concentrate my attention, then it would abound. Never however did it attain this overabounding degree, this exuberant mightiness, so beyond comprehending and which left me shattered and crying. Or if it did attain it, I still had my mistrust of what had so strangely generated a disturbance to which those juvenile intellectual games would be party. In the ecstasy that had enveloped Hansi and me, first engaged were our naked loins, then a boundless love which would not be satisfied until our loins were bared, until they were freed unlimitedly. That abolishing of limits which left the two of us lost appeared to me more profound than the sermon of the priest in the chapel, appeared to me more holy. I saw there the greatness of God where I had always seen only the limitlessness, the unmeasurableness, the mindless frenzy of love. So it was that in my distress I embraced Hansi's buttocks, realizing that I was no less thoroughly banished from the joy they had given me than if it had been through divine malediction. But in that unhappiness, which was not deep, I had strength enough to tell myself, I love Hansi's behind, I love it also for being damned by God's curse; in my sickness I deride that malediction, which deifies these buttocks so profoundly. They are divine if I kiss them, if I know that Hansi likes to feel my lips touching them. Thereupon I drew up the covers, and the object of my impotent passion was gone from sight. Like a descending blade, sleep and sudden dreaming sundered me from the world where I was really living. The naked body beside me became many bodies, dancing bodies composing a kind of round, not just lewd, aggressive, but beckoning to the pleasure of devouring as much as to that of fornicating, and, beckoning to the lowest, vilest pleasure, at the same time grinning in the direction of suffering, in the direction of the stranglehold of death. That roundelay proclaimed that ugliness, old age, excrement are less rare than beauty, elegance, the glamour of youth. I had a sensation of waters on the rise: the waters were those horrors, and soon there would be no further refuge to take before their mounting: as the drowning man's throat opens to the enormity of the waters, I would succumb to the power of malediction, to the power of woe.

My nightmare did not develop as smoothly as that, and while its beginning was to remain in my mind, I have forgotten how it ended. Fifty years later all I remember is having been struck by it at the time, when I was twenty. I do not remember the dream itself, but rather the feeling it left me with and which, there can be no doubt, I afterwards systematized as best I could. I associated the image I still had of divinity with that, equally violent, of Hansi's voluptuousness, and both of these I associated with those abominations whose potency, whose horribleness were infinite. I had in the days of my godliness meditated upon Christ crucified and upon the ungodliness of His wounds. The torturing nausea which came from an over-indulgence in sensual pleasure had introduced me to that awful confusion in which no sensation existed without being pitched to deliriousness.

My moral insensibility, my moral torpor had made

astonishing progress. As if, soaked in morphine, my nerves had ceased to feel anything. To religion, which I had at first thought was wreaking havoc in me, I simply did not give any more thought. The delight I gave her, the desire for pleasure which opened her to me, the sweetness of seeing emerge the profound nakedness of her body, of stripping it bare and of waxing excited over it; these had substituted themselves for the trembling, the convulsive starts and for the vision imparted to me by divine presence, which in other days had spoken to me, had called to me, had tortured me.

News soon reached me from my mother. I was not missing her, and when her letters told me, in the baldest terms, of the life she was leading in Egypt, it at first hardly scandalized me at all; instead of being upset, I was amused. Me too, I said to myself, and Hansi too . . . My mother was becoming frantic, uncontrolled . . . but she told me that she was happy: delighted, she said, instead of settling down, to be becoming a little more unsettled with every passing day. I might have guessed her reason for writing to me; but I admired her, I envied her, and I thanked her for my happiness.

In one place she wrote:

Your father kept me from going off the deep end. Through a feigned respectability I tried to cover up his drunkenness. Today, in Egypt, where I am unknown, where, except when I pick up my mail at the *poste restante*, I even go under an assumed name, I am slowly becoming the talk of the town: my fame is such that I am pointed at in the street. I make less noise getting drunk than your father used to . . . but I'm seen everywhere with women. Rhea is moderating me, just imagine it! She entreats me to go out with men. So I go out with men. It's worse still, says Rhea. So that evening I go out with her: they throw us out of a restaurant, our behaviour was improper. I shouldn't tell you so, but the lovely Hansi gives me to understand that my last letter made you laugh. I ask, I need, no more. The road ahead of me leads downwards, and I have stopped dragging my feet; the more speed I gather, the more heartily I laugh and the more admirable I find myself. I admire myself for writing to you as I do, and I am enchanted to think that my letter is worthy of my correspondent.

    Your scapegrace mother, thrilled to know that you are merry and that, so I am informed by Hansi, you are no less a dreamer than I.

Madeleine

Up until not long before such a letter would have cast me into despair. It frightened me, but the next instant I felt thankful to be living this way, in this 'dream' world, for me unfamiliar but to which I was committed by my mother's insolence. At that point I cherished an attractive image of my mother, a fairly accurate one; she had the right to conduct herself as she did, I could conceive of nobody of greater energy, of greater forcefulness: she was audacity itself and conscious of the abyss she was defying. I wrote back to her at once:

    You frighten me, Mother, but I like being afraid, since the more afraid I am, the more I love you. But it saddens me to think that I am denied one hope: my audacity will never give you the feeling of being outdone. *Of this I am ashamed*, and yet the thought is a pleasurable one for me. The only audacity reserved for me is to be proud of you, to be proud of your way of life, and to follow you *from afar*. But I am just beginning to feel uncomfortable about the relative reasonableness of Hansi's behaviour. Without telling her so I laugh at it — along with you; but I'd not have either the power or the inclination to corrupt her.

To this the reply was the postscript to a gay letter written in the same vein as the first.

'Alone, you'd not be able to corrupt Hansi: your error is to prefer pleasure to perversity. Perhaps, on some far-off day, we'll give each other a hand.'

I ought to have weighed the unhappy implications of that proposal. But how could I have discerned them? Today my rashness surprises me. My desires were urging me in all directions at once. Like Hansi, I naively wished to keep my pleasure at a safe distance from those suddenly attacking, distress-laden moods that the unhealthy inventions of vice are alone able to satisfy. Like Hansi, I feared such inventions. But Hansi, who often liked to come within a hair's-breadth of vice, was incapable of it, precisely because she knew that at the right moment she would back off. Vice fascinated me, maintaining me, in my eagerness for the worst, with my tongue hanging out and dry from thirst. Finally, though, I would do as she did and retreat, but I was never certain beforehand of being able to. I even had my experience to tell me that I had never known how to back off in time. I loved Hansi, and I loved the desire she had for continuous pleasure, the distaste she had for vice (as if voluptuousness could endure as an intellectual pleasure, but not as a physical pleasure without degenerating into vice). I understood it too late. Hansi's appetites were never insatiable: she wanted no clouds in the happiness she cherished, and she would never have sought it, as the depraved do, in unhappiness. Our happiness was precarious, it rested on a misunderstanding. I would tell her what I believed I thought, that I was in essential agreement with her, but at the same time I was writing to my mother in response to the lines I ought to have recognized as fraught with danger: 'Your scheme regarding our red-haired beauty sent a wonderful thrill racing up my spine. Of fear? Of delight? I do not know. I'd like to join hands with you.'

Having my mother at a distance made me strong, I now had a

very faraway image of her, and I lived in the present. The present, the 'red-haired beauty' whose long legs and golden fleece I would at nightfall bring forth from mists of lace. Hansi would cover me with needling kisses. I no longer found her so timid. But my mother used a separate page upon which to tell me what was not to fall into my tall redhead's hands: 'Our beauty is never going to know', she wrote, 'that the mind's pleasure, fouler than the body's, is purer and the only one whose edge never dulls. Vice, in my view, is like the mind's dark radiance, which blinds and of which I am dying. Corruption is the spiritual cancer reigning in the depths of things. As fast as I debauch myself I sense my lucidity grow, and the steady breakdown of my nerves is nothing else in me than a havoc whose source is my innermost thinking. I am writing but I am drunk, and Rhea, underneath the table, is bedevilling me. I am not jealous of the beauty but I regret having to feel that she is more reasonable than Rhea.'

Hansi was receiving letters from my mother at the same time, letters whose hilarious exuberance kept Hansi from minding their incongruity. They were similar to the main part of those being addressed to me.

Hansi had been fascinated by my mother from the beginning, but had quickly felt afraid of her. She laughed at that fear; yet, while looking forward to my mother's return, like me she could not help but be apprehensive about it.

One day she showed me what she had written in answer to her.

Pierre impatiently awaits the return of his mother, as I do that of my mistress. (On the eve of our first meeting Hansi had tasted her embraces.) Were I not every night in your child's arms . . . I would dream of yours, or of your girlish bosom. But every day I must yield myself afresh to the torrential dream of Pierre (and likewise not a day goes by but I renew the call to which his torment replies). I am so happy because of you that I know I ought to repay you in

kind, but the happiness I owe you is beyond anything I
could bestow; in your arms I shall laugh out of laughing
gratitude, ashamed of the pleasures Pierre and I give each
other, happy for the pleasures to which an insatiable desire
opens you, a desire which is wedded to mine as our two
bodies were as lovers. I kiss you and ask Pierre's
forgiveness. To think the thoughts I am thinking now is to
betray him, but just as in loving him I am certain of being
faithful to you, I remain faithful to him as, thinking of you, I
slip my tongue between your teeth. But you in your turn
will forgive me if, when you arrive, I withhold my body
from your kisses, for I reserve for Pierre what is most
precious of all. To be deprived of a pleasure is for me to
become ill, but to deprive myself for the sake of your little
Pierre is a bit to deprive myself for yours, and that is to
make myself more than happy.

I made no comment; I thanked Hansi, but inside I thought
that instead of making me happy, this refusal, coated over
with conceits, was saddening me. I would have preferred to
have Hansi amuse herself with my mother from time to time. I
hated the idea of drinking with my mother, in the way she had
liked us to drink together, and of then gradually drifting
towards the precipice. But despite the heaviness those letters
sometimes — not always — left in my heart, I loved them. At
no point had I forgotten that Hansi was my mother's mistress.
That relationship had pleased me from the first, and now I
would have liked it to be renewed and to last. Reading out the
letter she had written, Hansi had stirred me deeply. But its
close, though foreseen, had disappointed me; my one
consolation was the thought that Hansi did not intend to
withhold the entirety of herself, her body but not her mouth. I
took cynical pleasure thinking my mother would kiss Hansi in
front of me. If I favoured an intimacy based on such lines it

was all the more so because refusal of the body limited what, if unlimited, would have filled me with terror.

I had an as yet distant feeling that my will was slowly going to pieces and that my mother's return was to be the cyclone that would make a hideous shambles of everything. But the effect of the irresponsible phrases in Hansi's letter, at the moment of listening to them read aloud, was to excite me.

'I'd like to see your red-haired beauty,' I said to her.

Sly-eyed, she took the hint. I told myself that at bottom we were two of a kind, and that the presence or simply the mentioning of either of her girlfriends was enough, coming at the crucial instant, to incline her to 'dreaming'. At five o'clock that afternoon she admitted me to the mysteries within the 'golden gate', and it was not until three in the morning that the rites ended and the gate closed. Lulu, who served us and whom we invited to join us, asked me, the next day, what had got us into such a state.

'I can't tell you what it was like,' Lulu was saying. 'Hansi lying there before me, her head arched back, the whites of her eyes showing. You'd never have kissed her while I was there. Caressing her, you'd never uncovered her so far up. You were oblivious to everything.'

'I'd become oblivious to you . . .'

Lulu smiled at me, she lifted her skirt. Her mischievousness and her niceness, the pure lines of her legs and the charm of her indecency, and finally her seriousness, her unobtrusiveness, suggested some figure from the *Thousand and One Nights*, suggested still more the idea of a rich and lovely young girl whom an evil spell, metamorphosing her into a housemaid, had turned into the incarnation of wanton desire.

My attitude came down to that of a man who is well off,

possessing youth, money and good looks, considering the world and the people in it as made for the satisfaction of his extravagant desires. I now knew where happiness lay, a happiness to which unhappiness itself — and, naively, I was proud of this knowledge — added, like the colour black to the palette, a possibility of depth. I was happy, I was at the height of happiness. In the daytime I turned my attention to this insipid world, but only on condition that I got some puerile or intellectual satisfaction out of it — to be savoured with irony. At day's end the fête would begin again. Hansi, who in Lulu's presence had never permitted anything except when under the influence of drink, did at last agree to some compromises.

'After all, it's silly of me to feel uncomfortable,' she said.

She opened a closet and took out a certain number of dresses. Lulu came in and helped her put on one of them, a dress of transparent material. When the two women returned from the bathroom Hansi had herself admired and Lulu pointed out the slits which gave a clear view of what the dress veiled thinly. All this was very novel, and the change delighted me.

But after having relished the effect she had produced, Hansi's mood shifted.

'It's amusing,' she said, 'provided one stops in time.'

'Much more amusing,' I concurred.

'Promise me, Pierre, that you'll stop in time! I was at a loose end this afternoon, I turned to Lulu and it turned out a success. I didn't have the feeling I was being unfaithful to you.'

'On the contrary, Hansi, I'm sure we are going to love one another more fully tonight.'

'And so am I sure, but I refuse to do what Lulu would like. Leave us now, Lulu. I sense Pierre's impatience — and my own. I'll ring for you soon.'

Even before she heard the door close, Hansi, lying in my arms, had begun to run wild.

'I love you,' she said, 'and you are right, I am going to love you more fully than ever, I even believe I am going to make you happier.'

We sank so far into the abyss of pleasure that I said to Hansi, 'A little while ago I didn't know who you were, and yet now I love you a little more than is possible: you tear me apart and I believe I am tearing you apart, to the soul . . .'

'I'd like to have something to drink before going to sleep,' Hansi said to me. 'Let's disentangle ourselves, I am sure we shall be in the same state of grace as when Lulu left. Dress yourself and hand me my dress.'

She smiled as she got into that dress, a parody of an article of clothing, but she arranged it in such a way as to seem decent.

'I implore you, Pierre,' said Hansi, 'even if you desire me as much as a little while ago, don't come near me. You know how afraid I am of games.' But it was with a laugh that she added, in a voice altered by tension and as she placed her cheek very tenderly upon my thigh, 'If even so I were to behave . . . a little badly, you wouldn't scold me? But don't overdo it. Tonight it's my turn to be spoiled — all right? Although . . . just don't make me go farther than I want to. Don't forget: I've almost always said no . . .' Then, all of a sudden full of roguish gaiety, she said, 'It will probably be enormous fun, since we are scared!'

'Maybe you could readjust your dress, but maybe there's no point in bothering,' I said to her, peering at her garment which seemed once again in disarray.

'What am I to say? I'm in a mood you haven't seen me in before, but I should have thought that would please you.'

'I'd never have thought it would please me so much, but it pleases me precisely because you are uneasy, like I am, and because you wouldn't go the whole way.'

'You sound hoarse, and so do I. I hear Lulu coming.'

Lulu placed the bottles in the ice. At first I noticed nothing in particular about her apart from the smile, more knowing, more covert, than her usual one.

'Lulu,' Hansi said to her, 'we are going to have a good time today. A kiss?'

Lulu slipped down on the sofa and, since she had in the meantime put on a dress which was slit like the other, as she slipped down the panels opened in such a way as to reveal her naked behind when she opened her mouth to Hansi's voracious tongue.

But Hansi pushed Lulu away almost immediately, and stood up.

'That makes me thirsty,' she said.

'May I kiss him?' Lulu asked, looking at me.

Furious, Hansi confined herself to glaring at her.

'But, Hansi,' Lulu said, 'no one is paying the least bit of attention to him.'

'That is a shame,' said Hansi; then, to me, 'come into my arms.'

She surrendered so completely during that kiss that Lulu, participating in our ecstasy, lay back in the armchair nearby and shuddered.

Hansi rose, went over to her, kicked her.

'We want to drink,' she said, 'we are terribly thirsty.' And she added, 'Unbearably thirsty, Lulu.'

Getting up, I fixed my eyes upon the huge glasses on the tray, which Lulu hurriedly filled with champagne.

I was revelling in my restlessness.

'I want you to be touching me while I am drinking,' Hansi said to Lulu.

Half squatting, Lulu placed both her hands on Hansi who, standing up, leaned against her; gazing at me, Hansi opened herself to me in a gaze which was at the same time contracting ever so slightly.

Looking at her, I drank.

Lulu drank, then refilled the glasses. We were all three very quiet.

'I am going to have another glass,' Lulu said. 'I don't want you to be drunk before I am. Then, with Monsieur's leave, Madame shall drink from my hands . . .'

We fell silent again. Again Hansi leaned herself against Lulu; Hansi's legs were outrageously far apart. She drank greedily, but paused in her drinking at the same moment I did and rested, her eyes fastened gravely upon mine. The atmosphere was one of solemnity. It was unbreathable.

When we removed into the dining-room we were already drunk. But at the same time we were silent. I waited. Hansi waited, and as I examined Lulu it seemed to me that of the three of us, she was the most in trouble. Through slit skirts showed the possibility and, who knows the imminence of violent disorder. But it was enough to do up a button for Hansi's dress to gape at the neck no longer. We sat down to the cold supper lying ready on the table.

[*At this point the text becomes difficult to follow. The three characters drift into a paroxysmal orgy, and Georges Bataille seems to hesitate throughout between the crudest, the most direct descriptive vocabulary and the circumlocutions he has been employing since the opening pages of the manuscript. For some additions, appearing as notes, a definite place has not been assigned, and several passages, bracketed but not deleted, are uncertain. In the absence of a final draft of the novel's conclusion, we cannot arbitrarily decide in the writer's stead, and choose one version over another. We are therefore giving résumés — in italics — of these last sixteen pages, between those résumés inserting the most important among the legible passages.*]

Pierre, Hansi and Lulu, their frenzy having subsided, fall asleep from exhaustion. Pierre wakes in the middle of the night. Lulu's face shows a mark left by Hansi's riding crop.

I slept badly. When in the middle of the night I awoke I saw that we were in the dining-room. With my return to consciousness I was brought to realize the meaning of the unusual furnishings of the room, against whose walls stood a continuous silk-covered sofa. This very wide sofa was designed for collective revels; there was a serving hatch to enable Lulu, if need be, to clear away the table without leaving the room. I wondered at my own naivety: we had already made love on this vast sofa, but it never occurred to me that Hansi had installed it for that purpose. Drowsing, confronted by the nakedness of those women sprawled in disorder, for a moment I felt as though I were in the midst of a distressing dream: it was not an unpleasant dream, but there was no getting out of it. By the faint light coming from a sky where the moon emerged only now and again from behind clouds, I had been able to catch a glimpse of Lulu's face, disfigured by the stripe it bore. Hansi had done something she had told me she disliked doing, and which I had often regretted that she disliked, but the furnishings provided for such frolics proved that she was accustomed to them. There was nothing I felt I wished to blame her for, I was in love with her and I had found the very greatest pleasure in playing those games; before becoming actually familiar with them, I had liked the idea of them, but when my taste had first made itself felt it had been under baleful auspices, in solitude before my father's photographs or during frightening scenes involving Rhea, my mother and me. I was once again in the frame of mind my self-abuse would bring on and that I had been in after meeting Rhea. I was feverish, and since coming to Hansi's this was the first time I felt anguish clutch my heart.

In that state I went off to sleep again, then awoke anew: Hansi was crying on the sofa. She was face down on the sofa and crying. Or rather, biting one of her fists, she was holding back from crying. I went towards her and quietly asked her if she would come along with me into her bedroom and lie down. She did not answer but she got up and followed me. Once in bed she began to tremble, still holding back her tears. The thought crossed my mind that Lulu's sleeping body, her face slashed, still lay in the dining-room.

'Hansi,' I said, 'we'll never do this any more.'

She made no reply, but now gave free rein to her tears.

It was only after quite a while that, in a stifled voice, Hansi said to me, 'I have to give you an explanation, Pierre, but it is awful.'

Then she went on. 'I did it despite myself and now I have the feeling everything is ruined . . . Your mother . . .'

And she was shaken by sobs.

'It's too hard . . . I just can't any longer. I love you too much, but everything's done for. Go away.'

She cried on and on. At last, still sobbing, she spoke to me: 'You know that I was, *that I am* your mother's mistress, and games like those we have just indulged in, those, as you know, are what she has gone in for. Right up to the day she left she worked on me. It wasn't very difficult. Lulu was always here in the house. She had been my mistress for a long time, in the wretched servant's disguise she liked wearing; this affair grew up out of the games we played as children when Lulu, who had a violent character, would force me to beat and humiliate her. There had always been something insane about our doings together, Lulu dominated me, she imposed her will upon me. She would keep at me until I was beside myself. That was the moment when I would go into the cold rage you saw me in a short while ago. Your mother had no trouble making an ally out of Lulu, above all because, since I was unwilling to leave her, Lulu immediately realized that the parties your mother proposed represented her one chance for getting what she wanted out of me. As I did when you and I fell in love, I agreed to nothing beyond playing housemaid and mistress. But the worst began the day your mother, having got me drunk, got what she was after: I behaved that

day the same way I did last night. And I whipped Lulu while
your mother watched.'

*Pierre's mother had thus managed to involve Hansi in collective
debauches. And now, about to come back, she has notified her of what she
wants: everything is to be resumed, but this time in the presence of Pierre.*

'I refused,' Hansi told me.

'Of course,' I said, 'of course!'

But within my distress lay concealed the desire to reply to
my mother's fantastic proposal, not to spurn that prodigy of
unhappiness and distress. I loved Hansi, but in her I loved the
possibility of loving to the point beyond return; and, however
much I might dread my mother's dark carousings, from what
in this dread I could imagine to be their sweetness, blended
with the prospect of suffering and the intimation of death . . . I
had no sooner exclaimed those two words 'of course!' than I
sensed not only that my mother had me at her mercy, but that
I yearned for the disaster towards which she was steering me
from so far away. At the idea of losing Hansi sorrow was rising
in my chest, I was already in tears. But the remembrance of
Hansi's night-long excesses caused me to say inside myself,
'Neither will you, Hansi, be able to stand on the brink, the
same whirlwind will carry you over it.'

Pierre and Hansi return to where they have left Lulu.

'We intend to cheer ourselves up in front of you,' Hansi said to
her. 'For us everything is over with, his mother is coming
back. Rejoice, we are going to suffer, and we shall help you
share our suffering, so as to change it into joy.'

Lulu had trouble speaking. 'When is she due back?' she asked.

'We don't know, but madness has already taken over the house. The worse you behave the better you will satisfy what ails us.'

A little later, Lulu said this to me, 'Have pity, demand the worst from me. Is there nothing nastier I can do? I am grief-stricken. Pierre, do you know what your mother did for her amusement in Cairo? What she did to men at night in dirty side-streets? You have no idea how proud of her I would be if I were you, silently proud. She is aboard ship now. But it was every single night — I cannot speak without opening my lips, and now I am happy. Or rather I would be happy if, dying, I were kissing your mother's feet.'

Hansi and I, we both reached for her, clutched her, impelled by a sort of painful and feverish convulsion. Hansi at last let herself go and the thought of my mother produced in her the same exhausting, woeful, wounding ecstasy as in Lulu and as in me. We were no longer even drinking anything. We were in pain, and from being in that pain we derived a bitter joy.

Depressed the whole day, we hovered between a light sleep and something that was not so much dormant pain as a delight which was the dregs of pleasure. We were confined in the part of the flat that Hansi called the sanctuary, which, from inside, was easily isolated from the rest, and included Hansi's bedroom, the bathroom and the big dining-room. Sometimes we lay down on a rug, sometimes on a sofa. We were naked, dishevelled, hollow-eyed, but those eyes seemed to have a beauty, telling of some broken mechanism that sometimes, at the unexpected touch of some switch, gave forth the thunder of a spent storm. Suddenly we heard a knocking in the hallway.

The knock had been at the outer entrance to the bathroom. The person who had knocked was plainly familiar with the plan of the house. As far as I knew, the hour was late. I got into my bathrobe and opened the door. At the door there was nobody, but at the other end of the long hallway, just visible in the faint overhead light, I made out two women who seemed to be undressing — or else dressing. The operation concluded, from afar I saw that they were both wearing masks under superb top hats. They were indeed dressed, but only in a chemise and ample silk drawers. They walked straight towards and past me, entered without a word. Having shut the door, one of them latched it, then they proceeded through the bathroom, through the bedroom, into the dining-room, where they woke up my mistress and her maid. Their carnival masks and make-up prevented me from telling them apart. I understood at once that one must be my mother, Rhea the other; and that if they avoided speaking, it was to heighten my distress, if that were possible. And they wanted to provoke a distress in me that would match their own. One of them spoke in Lulu's ear, and she repeated aloud what was being said to her. It was mainly at me, so it seemed, that the speech was aimed. It was aimed at my distress. Since the night before they had been spending their time in games which had left them no less weary than we. Nothing remained of the insolent gaiety those four women had possessed — and by now there was no doubt in my mind that our visitors were Rhea and my mother. They had not, they said, brought along other women — or other men — who might have distracted them from an element which was creating such a profound disturbance in them.

All of a sudden I found myself opposite my mother, she had drawn away from the others, withdrawn from their embraces, had torn off her mask, and she was looking at me obliquely, as

though with that oblique smile she had freed herself of the
weight which was crushing her to death.

She said, 'You have not known me. You have not been able
to get at me.'

'I have known you,' I said to her. 'And now you are lying
here in my arms. I shall not be more worn out when the
moment comes for me to breathe my final breath.'

'Kiss me,' she said, 'to stop yourself thinking. Put your
mouth to my mouth. And now be happy for the instant, as if I
had not ruined myself, as if I were not destroyed. I want to
lead you into this world of death and corruption where you
already sense that I am imprisoned; I always knew you would
love it too. I would like us to go out of our minds together. I
would like to drag you with me as I die. A brief instant of the
madness I shall give you is better, is it not, than freezing in a
universe of stupidity? I want to die, I have burned my boats.
Your corruption was my handiwork: I gave you what was
purest and most intense in me, the desire to love that which
tears the clothes off my body, and that alone. This time, they
are all my clothes.'

While I watched, my mother removed her chemise and her
drawers. She lay down naked.

'I know now', said she, 'that you are going to outlive me and
that, by outliving me, you will betray an abominable mother.
But if later on you think back upon the embrace which will
soon unite you with me, do not forget the reason why I slept with
women. This is not the moment to talk about the wreck you
had for a father; was that a man? You know that I used to like
to laugh, it may be that I am not yet done laughing; you'll not
know until the last instant whether I have laughed at you . . .
No, I don't want you to answer. I no longer know if it's that I
am afraid or that I love you too much. Let me reel with you in
that joy, that certainty of a destruction more complete, more
violent than any desire. The pleasure engulfing you is already
so great that I am able to speak to you; what you feel now will

take you to the failure of your senses. The moment you expire
I shall leave, and never again will you see her who waited for
you, only to give you her last breath. Ah, grit your teeth, my
son, you resemble your cock, this cock streaming with rage
which clenches my desire like a fist.'

MADAME
EDWARDA

PREFACE

> Death is the most terrible of all things; and
> to maintain its works is what requires the
> greatest of all strength.
>
> *Hegel*

The author of this book has himself insisted upon the gravity of what he has to say*. Nonetheless, it would seem advisable to underscore the seriousness of it, if only because of the widespread custom of making light of those writings that deal with the subject of sexual life. Not that I hope — or intend to try — to change anything in customs that prevail. But I invite the reader of this preface to turn his thoughts for a moment to the attitude traditionally observed towards pleasure (which, in sexual play, attains a wild intensity, an insanity) and towards pain (finally assuaged by death, of course, but which, before that, dying winds to the highest pitch). A combination of conditions leads us to entertain a picture of mankind as it ought to be, and in that picture man appears at no less great a remove from extreme pleasure as from extreme pain: the most ordinary social restrictions and

* Bataille wrote Madame Edwarda under the pseudonym, *Pierre Angélique*. See publisher's note.

prohibitions are, with equal force, aimed some against sexual life, some against death, with the result that each has come to comprise a sanctified domain, a sacred area which lies under religious jurisdiction. The greater difficulties began when the prohibitions connected with the circumstances attending the disappearance of a person's life were alone allowed a serious character, whilst those touching the circumstances which surround the coming into being of life — the entirety of genital activity — tended to be taken unseriously. It is not a protest against the profound general inclination that I have in mind: this inclination is another expression of the human destiny which would make man's reproductive organs the object of laughter. But this laughter, which accentuates the pleasure–pain opposition (pain and death merit respect, whereas pleasure is derisory, deserving of contempt), also underscores their fundamental kinship. Man's reaction has ceased to betoken respect: his laughter is the sign of aversion, of horror. Laughter is the compromise attitude man adopts when confronted by something whose appearance repels him, but which at the same time does not strike him as particularly grave. And thus when eroticism is considered with gravity, considered tragically, this represents a complete reversal of the ordinary situation.

I wish right away to make clear the total futility of those often-repeated statements to the effect that sexual prohibitions boil down to no more than prejudices which it is high time we get rid of. The shame, the modesty sensed in connection with the strong sensation of pleasure, would be, so the argument runs, mere proofs of backwardness and unintelligence. Which is the equivalent of saying that we ought to undertake a thorough housecleaning, set fire to our house and take to the woods, returning to the good old days of animalism, of devouring whoever we please and whatever ordures. Which is the equivalent of forgetting that what we call humanity, mankind, is the direct result of poignant, indeed violent impulses, alternately of revulsion and attraction, to which sensibility and intelligence are inseparably attached. But without wishing in any sense to gainsay the laughter that is roused by the idea or spectacle of indecency, we may legitimately return — partially return — to an attitude which came to be through the operation of laughter.

It is indeed in laughter that we find the justification for a form of castigation, of obloquy. Laughter launches us along the path that leads to the transforming of a prohibition's principle, of necessary and mandatory decencies, into an iron-clad hypocrisy, into a lack of understanding or an unwillingness to understand what is involved. Extreme licence wedded with a joking mood is accompanied by a refusal to take the underlying truth of eroticism seriously: by seriously I mean *tragically*.

I should like to make this preface the occasion of a pathetic appeal (in the strongest sense); for, in this little book, eroticism is plainly shown as opening directly out upon a certain vista of anguish, upon a certain lacerating conscious-ness of distress. Not that I think it surprising that, most often, the mind shuts itself off to this distress and to itself, and so to speak turning its back, in its stubbornness becomes a caricature of its own truth. If man needs lies . . . why, then let man lie. There are, after all, men enough who are proud to drown themselves in the indifference of the anonymous mass . . . But there is also a will, with its puissant and wonderful qualities, to open wide the eyes, to see forthrightly and fully *what is happening, what is*. And there would be no knowing what is happening if one were to know nothing of the extremest pleasure, if one knew nothing of extremest pain.

Not let us be clear on this. Pierre Angélique is careful to say so: we know nothing, we are sunk in the depths of ignorance's darkness. But we can at least see what is deceiving us, what diverts us from knowledge of our distress, from knowing, more precisely, that joy is the same thing as suffering, the same thing as dying, as death.

What the hearty laugh screens from us, what fetches up the

bawdy jest, is the identity that exists between the utmost in pleasure and the utmost in pain: the identity between being and non-being, between the living and the death-stricken being, between the knowledge which brings one before this dazzling realization and definitive, concluding darkness. To be sure, it is not impossible that this truth itself evokes a final laugh; but our laughter here is absolute, going far beyond scorning ridicule of something which may perhaps be repugnant, but disgust for which digs deep under our skin.

If we are to follow all the way through to its last the ecstasy in which we lose ourselves in love-play, we have got constantly to bear in mind what we set as ecstasy's immediate limit: horror. Not only can the pain I or others feel, drawing me closer to the point where horror will force me to recoil, enable me to reach the state where joy slips into delirium; but when horror is unable to quell, to destroy the object that attracts, then horror *increases* the object's power to charm. Danger paralyzes; but, when not overpoweringly strong, danger can arouse desire. We do not attain to ecstasy save when before the however remote prospect of death, of that which destroys us.

Man differs from animal in that he is able to experience certain sensations that wound and melt him to the core. These sensations vary in keeping with the individual and with his specific way of living. But, for example, the sight of blood, the odor of vomit, which arouse in us the dread of death, sometimes introduce us into a kind of nauseous state which hurts more cruelly than pain. Those sensations associated with the supreme giving-way, the final collapse, are unbearable. Are there not some persons who claim to prefer death to touching an even completely harmless snake? There seems to exist a domain where death signifies not only decease and disappearance, but the unbearable process by which we disappear *despite ourselves* and everything we can do, even though, *at all costs*, we *must not* disappear. It is precisely this *despite ourselves*, this *at all costs* which distinguish the moment of extreme joy and of indescribable but miraculous ecstasy. If there is nothing that surpasses our powers and our understanding, if we do not acknowledge something greater than ourselves, greater than we are *despite ourselves*, something which *at all costs must* not be, then we do not reach the *insensate* moment towards which we strive with all that is in our power and which at the same time we exert all our power to stave off.

Pleasure would be a puny affair were it not to involve this leap, this staggering overshooting of the mark which common sense fixes — a leap that is not confined alone to sexual ecstasy, one that is known also to the mystics of various religions, one that above all Christian mystics experienced, and experienced in this same way. The act whereby being — existence — is bestowed upon us is an *unbearable* surpassing of being, an act no less unbearable than that of dying. And since, in death, being is taken away from us at the same time it is given us, we must seek for it in the feeling of dying, in those unbearable moments when it seems to us that we are dying because the existence in us, during these interludes, exists through nothing but a sustaining and ruinous excess, when the fullness of horror and that of joy coincide.

Our minds' operations as well never reach their final culmination save in excess. What, leaving aside the representation of excess, what does truth signify if we do not see that which exceeds sight's possibilities, that which it is unbearable to see as, in ecstasy, it is unbearable to know pleasure? what, if we do not think that which exceeds thought's possibilities?. . .[1]

At the further end of this pathetic meditation — which, with a cry, undoes itself, unravelling to drown in self-repudiation, for it is unbearable to its own self — we rediscover God. That is the meaning, that is the enormity of this *insensate* — this mad — book: a book which leads God upon the stage, God in the plenitude of His attributes; and this God, for all that, is what? A public whore, in no way different from any other public whore. But what mysticism could not

say (at the moment it began to pronounce its message, it
entered it — entered its trance), eroticism does say: God is
nothing if He is not, in every sense, the surpassing of God: in
the sense of common everyday being, in the sense of dread,
horror and impurity, and, finally, in the sense of nothing . . .
We cannot with impunity incorporate the very word into our
speech which surpasses words, the word *God*; directly we do
so, this word, surpassing itself, explodes past its defining,
restrictive limits. That which this word is, stops nowhere, is
checked by nothing, it is everything and, everywhere, is
impossible to overtake anywhere. And he who so much as
suspects this instantly falls silent. Or, hunting for a way out,
and realizing that he seals himself all the more inextricably
into the impasse, he searches within himself for that which,
capable of annihilating him, renders him similar to God,
similar to nothing.[2]

In the course of the indescribable journey upon which this
most incongruous of books invites us to embark, we may
perhaps make a few more discoveries.

For example, that, perchance, of happiness, of delight . . .

And here indeed joy does announce itself within the
perspective of death (thus is joy made to wear the mask of its
contrary, grief).

I am by no means predisposed to think that voluptuous
pleasure is the essential thing in this world. Man is more than
a creature limited to its genitals. But they, those inavowable
parts of him, teach him his secret.[3] Since intense pleasure
depends upon the presence of a deleterious vision before the
mind's eye, it is likely that we will be tempted to try to slink in
by some back way, doing our best to get at joy by a route that
keeps us as far away as possible from horror. The images
which quicken desire or provoke the critical spasm are usually
equivocal, *louche*: if it be horror, if it be death these images
present, they always present them guilefully. Even in Sade's
universe, death's terrible edge is deflected away from the self
and aimed at the partner, the victim, at the *other* — and,

contradictorily, Sade shows the other as the most eminently delightful expression of life. The sphere of eroticism is inescapably plighted to duplicity and ruse. The object which causes Eros to stir comes guised as other than truly it is. And so it does appear that, in the question of eroticism, it is the ascetics who are right. Beauty they call a trap set by the Devil: and only beauty excuses and renders bearable the need for disorder, for violence and for unseemliness which is the hidden root of love. This would not be the place to enter into a detailed discussion of transports whose forms are numerous and of which pure love slyly causes us to experience the most violent, driving the blind excess of life to the very edge of death. The ascetic's sweeping condemnation, admittedly, is blunt, it is craven, it is cruel, but it is squarely in tune with the fear and trembling without which we stray farther and farther away from the truth darkness sequesters. There is no warrant for ascribing to sexual love a pre-eminence which only the whole of life actually has, but, again, if we were to fail to carry the light to the very point where night falls, how should we know ourselves to be, as we are, the offspring, the effect of being hurling itself into horror? of being leaping headlong into the sickening emptiness, into the very nothingness which *at all costs* being has got to avoid. . .

Nothing, certainly, is more dreadful than this fall. How ludicrous the scenes of hell above the portals of churches must seem to us! Hell is the paltry notion God involuntarily gives us of Himself. But it requires the scale of limitless doom for us to discover the triumph of *being* — whence there has never lacked anything save consent to the impulse which would have been perishable. The nature of our being invites us of our own accord to join in the terrible dance whose rhythm is the one that ends in collapse, and which we must accept as it is and for what it is, knowing only the horror it is in perfect harmony with. If courage deserts us, if we give way, then there is no greater torture. And never does the moment of torture fail to arrive: how, in its absence, would we withstand and overcome it? But the unreservedly open spirit — open to death, to torment, to joy —, the open spirit, open and dying, suffering and dying and happy, stands in a certain veiled light: that light is divine. And the cry that breaks from a twisted mouth may perhaps twist him who utters it, but what he speaks is an immense *alleluia*, flung into endless silence, and lost there.

Georges Bataille

NOTES ON PREFACE

1 I regret having to add that this definition of being and of excess
cannot repose upon a philosophical basis, excess surpassing any
foundational basis: excess is no other than that whereby the being
is firstly and above all else conveyed beyond all circumscribing
restrictions. Being is also, doubtless, subject to certain other
limits: were this not so, we should not be able to speak (I too
speak, but as I speak I do not forget that not only will speech
escape me, but that it is escaping me now). These methodically
arranged sentences are possible (in a large measure possible since
excess is rather the exception than the rule, since excess is the
marvellous, the miraculous. . .; and excess designates the
attractive, if not the horrible, attraction, if not horror —
designates everything which is *more than what is*, than what exists),
but their impossibility is also fundamental. Thus: no tie ever
binds me, never am I enslaved, subjugated, I always retain my
sovereignty, a sovereignty only my death — which will
demonstrate my inability to limit myself to being without excess
— separates from me. I do not decline, I do not challenge
consciousness, lacking which I cannot write, but this hand that
writes is *dying* from the death promised unto it as its own, this
hand escapes the limits it accepts in writing (limits accepted by
the hand that writes, but refused by the hand that dies).

2 Here then is the primary theological attitude which would be
propounded by a man in whom laughter is illumination and who
disdains to impose limits, or to accept them: he who knows not
what a limit is. O mark the day when you read by a pebble of fire,
you who have waxed pale over the texts of the philosophers! How
may he express himself who bids these voices be still, unless it be
in a way that is not conceivable to them?

3 I could also point out, moreover, that excess is the very principle
and engine of sexual reproduction: indeed, *divine Providence* willed
that in its works its secret remain impenetrable! Were it then
possible to spare man nothing? The same day when he perceives

that the ground he stands on has fallen out from under his feet, he is told that it has been *providentially* removed! But would he have issue of his blasphemy, it is with blasphemy, it is in spitting defiance upon his own limitations, it is with blasphemy in his mouth that he makes himself God.

Anguish only is sovereign absolute. The sovereign is a king no more: it dwells low-hiding in big cities. It knits itself up in silence, obscuring its sorrow. Crouching thick-wrapped, there it waits, lies waiting for the advent of him who shall strike a general terror; but meanwhile and even so its sorrow scornfully mocks at all that comes to pass, at all there is.

There — I had come to a street corner — there a foul dizzying anguish got its nails into me (perhaps because I'd been staring at a pair of furtive whores sneaking down the stair of a urinal). A great urge to heave myself dry always comes over me at such moments. I feel I have got to make myself naked, or strip naked the whores I covet: it's in stale flesh's tepid warmth I always suppose I'll find relief. But this time I soothed my guts with the weaker remedy: I asked for a pernod at the counter, drank the glass in one gulp, and then went on and on, from zinc counter to zinc counter, drinking until . . . The night was done falling.

I began to wander among those streets — the propitious ones — which run between the Boulevard Poisonnière and the Rue Saint-Denis. Loneliness and the dark strung my drunken excitement tighter and tighter. I wanted to be laid as bare as was the night there in those empty streets: I slipped off my pants and moved on, carrying them draped over my arm. Numb, I coasted on a wave of overpowering freedom, I sensed that I'd got bigger. In my hand I held my straight-risen sex.

(The beginning is tough. My way of telling about these things is raw. I could have avoided that and still made it sound plausible. It would have seemed 'likely', detours would have been to my advantage. But this is how it has to be, there is no beginning by scuttling in sidewise. I continue . . . and it gets tougher.)

Not wanting trouble, I got back into my pants and headed toward the Mirrors. I entered the place and found myself in the light again. Amidst a swarm of girls, Madame Edwarda, naked, looked bored to death. Ravishing, she was the sort I had a taste for. So I picked her. She came and sat down beside me. I hardly took the time to reply when the waiter asked what it was to be, I clutched Edwarda, she surrendered herself: our two mouths met in a sickly kiss. The room was packed with men and women, and that was the wasteland where the game was played. Then, at a certain moment, her hand slid, I burst, suddenly, like a pane of glass shattering, flooding my clothes. My hands were holding Madame Edwarda's buttocks and I felt her break in two at the same instant: and in her starting, roving eyes, terror, and in her throat, a long-drawn whistled rasp.

Then I remembered my desire for infamy, or rather that it was infamous I had at all costs to be. I made out laughter filtering through the tumult of voices, of glare, of smoke. But nothing mattered any more. I squeezed Edwarda in my arms; immediately, icebound, I felt smitten within by a new shock. From very high above a kind of stillness swept down upon me and froze me. It was as though I were borne aloft in a flight of headless and unbodied angels shaped from the broad swooping of wings, but it was simpler than that. I became unhappy and felt painfully forsaken, as one is when in the presence of GOD. It was worse and more of a letdown than too much to drink. And right away I was filled with unbearable sadness to think that this very grandeur descending upon me was withering away the pleasure I hoped to have with Edwarda.

I told myself I was being ridiculous. Edwarda and I having exchanged not one word, I was assailed by a huge uneasiness. I couldn't breathe so much as a hint of the state I was in, a wintry night had locked round me. Struggling, I wanted to kick the table and send the glasses flying, to raise the bloody roof, but that table wouldn't budge, it must have been bolted to the floor. I don't suppose a drunk can ever have to face anything more comical. Everything swam out of sight. Madame Edwarda was gone, so was the room.

I was pulled out of my dazed confusion by an only too human voice. Madame Edwarda's thin voice, like her slender body, was obscene: 'I guess what you want is to see the old rag and ruin,' she said. Hanging on to the tabletop with both hands, I twisted around toward her. She was seated, she held one leg stuck up in the air, to open her crack yet wider she used fingers to draw the folds of skin apart. And so Madame Edwarda's 'old rag and ruin' loured at me, hairy and pink, just as full of life as some loathsome squid. 'Why,' I stammered in a subdued tone, 'why are you doing that?' 'You can see for yourself,' she said, 'I'm GOD.' 'I'm going crazy —' 'Oh, no you don't, you've got to see, look. . .' Her harsh, scraping voice mellowed, she became almost childlike in order to say, with a lassitude, with the infinite smile of abandon: 'Oh, listen, fellow! The fun I've had . . . '

She had not shifted from her position, her leg was still cocked in the air. And her tone was commanding: 'Come here.' 'Do you mean,' I protested, 'in front of all these people?' 'Sure,' she said, 'why not?' I was shaking, I looked at her: motionless, she smiled back so sweetly that I shook. At last, reeling, I sank down on my knees and feverishly pressed my lips to that running, teeming wound. Her bare thigh caressingly nudged my ear, I thought I heard a sound of roaring seasurge, it is the same sound you hear when you put your ear to a large conch shell. In the brothel's boisterous chaos and in the atmosphere of corroding absurdity I was breathing (it seemed to me that I was choking, I was flushed, I was sweating) I hung strangely suspended, quite as though at that same point we, Edwarda and I, were losing ourselves in a wind-freighted night, on the edge of the ocean.

I heard another voice, a woman's but mannish. She was a

robust and handsome person, respectably got up. 'Well now, my children,' in an easy, deep tone, 'up you go.' The second in command of the house collected my money. I rose and followed Madame Edwarda whose tranquil nakedness was already traversing the room. But this so ordinary passage between the close-set tables, through the dense press of clients and girls, this vulgar ritual of 'the lady going up' with the man who wants her in tow, was, at that moment, nothing short of an hallucinating solemnity for me: Madame Edwarda's sharp heels clicking on the tiled floor, the smooth advance of her long obscene body, the acrid smell I drank in, the smell of a woman in the throes of joy, of that pale body . . . Madame Edwarda went on ahead of me, raised up unto the very clouds . . . The room's noisy unheeding of her happiness, of the measured gravity of her step, was royal consecration and triumphal holiday: death itself was guest at the feast, was there in what whorehouse nudity terms the pig-sticker's stab
....
....
.... the mirrors wherewith the room's walls were everywhere sheathed and the ceiling too, cast multiple reflections of an animal coupling, but, at each least movement, our bursting hearts would strain wide-open to welcome 'the emptiness of heaven.'

Making that love liberated us at last. On our feet, we stood gazing soberly at each other: Madame Edwarda held me spellbound, never had I seen a prettier girl — nor one more naked. Her eyes fastened steadily upon me, she removed a pair of white silk stockings from a bureau drawer, she sat on the edge of the bed and drew them on. The delirious joy of being naked possessed her: once again she parted her legs, opened her crack, the pungent odor of her flesh and mine commingled flung us both into the same heart's utter exhaustion. She put on a white bolero, beneath a domino cloak she disguised her nakedness. The domino's hood cowled her head, a black velvet mask, fitted with a beard of lace, hid her face. So arrayed, she sprang away from me, saying: 'Now let's go.'

'Go? Do they let you go out?' I asked. 'Hurry up, fifi,' she replied gaily, 'you can't go out undressed.' She tossed me my clothes and helped me climb into them, and as she did so, from her caprice, there now and then passed a sly exchange, a nasty little wink darting between her flesh and mine. We went down a narrow stairway, encountered nobody but the chambermaid. Brought to a halt by the abrupt darkness of the street, I was startled to discover Edwarda rushing away, swathed in black. She ran, eluded me, was off, the mask she wore was turning her into an animal. Though the air wasn't cold, I shivered. Edwarda, something alien; above our heads, a starry sky, mad and void. I thought I was going to stagger, to fall, but didn't, and kept walking.

At that hour of the night the street was deserted. Suddenly gone wild, mute, Edwarda raced on alone. The Porte Saint-Denis loomed before her, she stopped. I stopped too, she waited for me underneath the arch — unmoving, exactly under the arch. She was entirely black, simply there, as distressing as an emptiness, a hole. I realized she wasn't frolicking, wasn't joking, and indeed that, beneath the garment enfolding her, she was mindless: rapt, absent. Then all the drunken exhilaration drained out of me, then I knew that She had not lied, that She was GOD. Her presence had about it the unintelligible out-and-out simplicity of a stone — right in the middle of the city I had the feeling of being in the mountains at nighttime, lost in a lifeless, hollow solitude.

I felt that I was free of Her — I was alone, as if face to face with black rock. I trembled, seeing before me what in all this world is most barren, most bleak. In no way did the comic horror of my situation escape me: She, the sight of whom petrified me now, the instant before had . . . And the transformation had occurred in the way something glides. In

Madame Edwarda, grief — a grief without tears or pain —
had glided into a vacant silence. Nonetheless, I wanted to find
out: this woman, so naked just a moment ago, who
lightheartedly had called me 'fifi' ... I crossed in her
direction, anguish warned me to go no farther, but I didn't
stop.

Unspeaking, she slipped away, retreating toward the pillar
on the left. Two paces separated me from that monumental
gate, when I passed under the stone overhead, the domino
vanished soundlessly. I paused, listening, holding my breath.
I was amazed that I could grasp it all so clearly: when she had
run off I had known that, no matter what, she had had to run,
to dash under the arch, and when she had stopped, that she
had been hung in a sort of trance, an absence, far out of range
and beyond the possibility of any laughter. I couldn't see her
any longer: a deathly darkness sank down from the vault.
Without having given it a second's thought, I 'knew' that a
season of agony was beginning for me. I consented to suffer, I
desired to suffer, to go farther, as far as the 'emptiness' itself,
even were I to be stricken, destroyed, no matter. I knew, I
wanted that knowing, for I lusted after her secret and did not
for one instant doubt that it was death's kingdom.

I moaned underneath the stone roof, then, terrified, I
laughed: 'Of all men, the sole to traverse the nothingness of
this arch!' I trembled at the thought she might fly, vanish
forever. I trembled as I accepted that, but from imagining it I
became crazed: I leaped to the pillar and spun round it. As
quickly I circled the other pillar on the right: she was gone.
But I couldn't believe it. I remained woestruck before the
portal and I was sinking into the last despair when upon the
far side of the avenue I spied the domino, immobile, just
faintly visible in the shadow: she was standing upright,
entranced still, planted in front of the ranged tables and chairs
of a café shut up for the night. I drew near her: she seemed
gone out of her mind, some foreign existence, the creature
apparently of another world and, in the streets of this one, less

than a phantom, less than a lingering mist. Softly she withdrew before me until in her retreat she touched against a table on the empty terrace. A little noise. As if I had waked her, in a lifeless voice she inquired: 'Where am I?'

Desperate, I pointed to the empty sky curved above us. She looked up and for a brief moment stood still, her eyes vague behind the mask, her gaze lost in the fields of stars. I supported her, it was in an unhealthy way she was clutching the domino, with both hands pulling it tight around her. She began to shake, to convulse. She was suffering. I thought she was crying but it was as if the world and the distress in her, strangling her, were preventing her from giving way to sobs. She wrenched away from me, gripped by a shapeless disgust; suddenly lunatic, she darted forward, stopped short, whirled her cloak high, displayed her behind, snapped her rump up with a quick jerk of her spine, then came back and hurled herself at me. A gale of dark savagery blew up inside her, raging, she tore and hammered at my face, hit with clenched fists, swept away by a demented impulse to violence. I tottered and fell. She fled.

I was still getting to my feet — was actually still on my knees — when she returned. She shouted in a raveled, impossible voice, she screamed at the sky and, horrified, her whirling arms flailing at vacant air: 'I can't stand any more,' she shrilled, 'but you, you fake priest. I shit on you—' That broken voice ended in a rattle, her outstretched hands groped blindly, then she collapsed.

Down, she writhed, shaken by respiratory spasms. I bent over her and had to rip the lace from the mask, for she was chewing and trying to swallow it. Her thrashings had left her naked, her breasts spilled through her bolero . . . I saw her flat, pallid belly, and above her stockings, her hairy crack yawned astart. This nakedness now had the absence of meaning and at the same time the overabundant meaning of death-shrouds. Strangest of all — and most disturbing — was the silence that ensnared Edwarda — owing to the pain she was in, further communication was impossible and I let myself be absorbed into this unutterable barrenness — into this black night hour of the being's core no less a desert nor less hostile than the empty skies. The way her body flopped like a fish, the ignoble rage expressed by the ill written on her features — cindered the life in me, dried it down to the lees of revulsion.

(Let me explain myself. No use laying it all up to irony when I say of Madame Edwarda that she is GOD. But GOD figured as a public whore and gone crazy — that, viewed through the optic of 'philosophy,' makes no sense at all. I don't mind having my sorrow derided if derided it has to be, he only will grasp me aright whose heart holds a wound that is an incurable wound, who never, for anything, in any way, would be cured of it . . . And what man, if so wounded, would ever be willing to 'die' of any other hurt?)

The awareness of my irreparable doom whilst, in that night, I knelt next to Edwarda was not less clear and not less imposing than it is now, as I write. Edwarda's sufferings dwelt in me like the quick truth of an arrow: one knows it will pierce the heart, but death will ride in with it. As I waited for annihilation, all that subsisted in me seemed to me to be the dross over which man's life tarries. Squared against a silence so black, something leaped in my heavy despair's midst. Edwarda's convulsions snatched me away from my own self, they cast my life into a desert waste 'beyond', they cast it there carelessly, callously, the way one flings a living body to the hangman.

A man condemned to die, when after long hours of waiting he arrives in broad daylight at the exact spot the horror is to be wrought, observes the preparations, his too full heart beats as though to burst; upon the narrow horizon which is his, every object, every face is clad in weightiest meaning and helps tighten the vice whence there is no time left him to escape. When I saw Madame Edwarda writhing on the pavement, I

entered a similar state of absorption, but I did not feel
imprisoned by the change that occurred in me. The horizon
before which Edwarda's sickness placed me was a fugitive
one, fleeing like the object anguish seeks to attain. Torn apart,
a certain power welled up in me, a power that would be mine
upon condition I agree to hate myself. Ugliness was invading
all of me. The vertiginous sliding which was tipping me into
ruin had opened up a prospect of indifference, of concerns, of
desires there was no longer any question: at this point, the
fever's desiccating ecstasy was issuing out of my utter inability
to check myself.

(If you have to lay yourself bare, then you cannot play with
words, trifle with slow-marching sentences. Should no one
unclothe what I have said, I shall have written in vain.
Edwarda is no dream's airy invention, the real sweat of her
body soaked my handkerchief, so real was she that, led on by
her, I came to want to do the leading in my turn. This book
has its secret, I may not disclose it. Now more words.)

Finally, the crisis subsided. Her convulsions continued a little
longer, but with waning fury, she began to breathe again, her
features relaxed, ceased to be hideous. Drained entirely of
strength, I lay full length down on the roadway beside her. I
covered her with my clothing. She was not heavy and I
decided to pick her up and carry her. One of the boulevard
taxi stands was not far away. She lay unstirring in my arms. It
took time to get there, thrice I had to pause and rest. She came
back to life as we moved along and when we reached the place
she wanted to be set down. She took a step and swayed. I
caught her, held her, held by me she got into the cab. Weakly,
she said: '. . . not yet . . . tell him to wait.' I told the driver to
wait. Half dead from weariness, I climbed in too and slumped
down beside Edwarda.

For a long time we remained without saying anything.
Madame Edwarda, the driver and I, not budging in our seats,

as though the taxi were rolling ahead. At last Edwarda spoke to me. 'I want him to take us to Les Halles.' I repeated her instructions to the driver, and we started off. He took us through dimly lit streets. Calm and deliberate, Edwarda loosened the ties of her cloak, it fell away from her. She got rid of the mask too, she removed her bolero and, for her own hearing, murmured: 'Naked as a beast.' She rapped on the glass partition, had the cab stop, and got out. She walked round to the driver and when close enough to touch him, said: 'You see . . . I'm bare-assed, Jack. Let's fuck.' Unmoving, the driver looked at that beast. Having backed off a short distance, she had raised her left leg, eager to show him her crack. Without a word and unhurriedly, the man stepped out of the car. He was thickset, solidly built. Edwarda twined herself around him, fastened her mouth upon his, and with one hand scouted about in his underwear. It was a long heavy member she dragged through his fly. She eased his trousers down to his ankles. 'Come into the back seat,' she told him. He sat down next to me. Stepping in after him, she mounted and straddled him. Carried away by voluptuousness, with her own hands she stuffed the hard stave into her hole. I sat there, lifeless and watching: her slithering movements were slow and cunning and plainly she gleaned a nerve-snapping pleasure from them. The driver retaliated, struggling with brute heaving vigor; bred of their naked bodies' intimacy, little by little that embrace strained to the final pitch of excess at which the heart fails. The driver fell back, spent and near to swooning. I switched on the overhead light in the taxi. Edwarda sat bolt upright astride the still stiff member, her head angled sharply back, her hair straying loose. Supporting her nape, I looked into her eyes: they gleamed white. She pressed against the hand that was holding her up, the tension thickened the wail in her throat. Her eyes swung to rights and then she seemed to grow easy. She saw me, from her stare, then, at that moment, I knew she was drifting home from the 'impossible' and in her nether depths I could discern a dizzying fixity. The milky outpouring travelling through her, the jet spitting from the root, flooding her with joy, came spurting out again in her very tears: burning tears streamed from her wide-open eyes. Love was dead in those eyes, they contained a daybreak aureate chill, a transparence wherein I read death's letters. And everything swam drowned in that dreaming stare: a long member, stubby fingers prying open fragile flesh, my anguish, and the recollection of scum-flecked lips — there was nothing which didn't contribute to that blind dying into extinction.

Edwarda's pleasure — fountain of boiling water, heartbursting furious tideflow — went on and on, weirdly, unendingly; that stream of luxury, its strident inflexion, glorified her being unceasingly, made her nakedness unceasingly more naked, her lewdness ever more intimate. Her body, her face swept in ecstasy were abandoned to the unspeakable coursing and ebbing, in her sweetness there hovered a crooked smile: she saw me to the bottom of my dryness, from the bottom of my desolation I sensed her joy's torrent run free. My anguish resisted the pleasure I ought to have sought. Edwarda's pain-wrung pleasure filled me with an exhausting impression of bearing witness to a miracle. My own distress and fever seemed small things to me. But that was what I felt, those are the only great things in me which gave answer to the rapture of her whom in the deeps of an icy silence I called 'my heart'.

Some last shudders took slow hold of her, then her sweatbathed frame relaxed — and there in the darkness sprawled the driver, felled by his spasm. I still held Edwarda up, my hand still behind her head, the stave slipped out, I helped her lie down, wiped her wet body. Her eyes dead, she offered no resistance. I had switched off the light, she was half asleep, like a drowsy child. The same sleepiness must have borne down upon the three of us, Edwarda, the driver and me.

(Continue? I meant to. But I don't care now. I've lost interest. I put down what oppresses me at the moment of writing: 'Would it all be absurd? Or might it make some kind of sense? I've made myself sick wondering about it. I awake in the morning — just the way millions do, millions of boys and

girls, infants and old men, their slumbers dissipated forever
. . . These millions, those slumbers have no meaning. A
hidden meaning? Hidden, yes, 'obviously'! But if nothing has
any meaning, there's no point in my doing anything. I'll beg
off. I'll use any deceitful means to get out of it, in the end I'll
have to let go and sell myself to meaninglessness, nonsense:
that is man's killer, the one who tortures and kills, not a
glimmer of hope left. But if there is a meaning? Today I don't
know what it is. Tomorrow? Tomorrow, who can tell? Am I
going then to find out what it is? No, I can't conceive of any
'meaning' other than 'my' anguish, and as for that, I know all
about it. And for the time being: nonsense. Monsieur
Nonsense is writing and understands that he is mad. It's
atrocious. But his madness, this meaninglessness — how
'serious' it has become all of a sudden! — might that indeed be
'meaningful'? [No, Hegel has nothing to do with a maniac
girl's 'apotheosis'.] My life only has a meaning insofar as I
lack one: oh, but let me be mad! Make something of all this he
who is able to, understand it he who is dying, and there the
living 'self is, knowing not why, its teeth chattering in the
lashing wind: the immensity, the night engulfs it and, all on
purpose, that living self is there just in order. . . 'not to know'.
But as for GOD? What have you got to say, Monsieur
Rhetorician? And you, Monsieur Godfearer? — GOD, if He
knew, would be a swine.* O Thou my Lord [in my distress I
call out unto my heart], O deliver me, make them blind! The
story — how shall I go on with it?)

But I am done.

From out of the slumber which for so short a space kept us
in the taxi, I awoke, the first to open his eyes . . . The rest is
irony, long, weary waiting for death . . .

* I said 'GOD, if He knew would be a swine.' He (He would I suppose be, at
that particular moment, somewhat in disorder, his peruke would sit all
askew) would entirely grasp the idea . . . but what would there be of the
human about him? Beyond, beyond everything. . . and yet farther, and even
farther still . . . HIMSELF, in an ecstasy, above an emptiness . . . And now? I
TREMBLE.

THE DEAD MAN

PREFACE

Georges Bataille died in 1962; *Le Mort* first appeared in 1964. He once showed me the manuscript — that would have been a good many years ago, in Orléans —: sheets of paper of an odd size, cut near to square, paper of the sort one found during the war when paper could not be found, and which had about it something I associate with French administration personnel, the dust in offices, blotters on desks. With wide margins to left and right, and with considerable blank space above and below, the writing, accumulated in the center of the page, seemed to hide there, to shrink: Bataille's small, spidery, yet neat handwriting, traced with a wire-fine pen. He only showed me the text: it was not given to me to read.

Did he mean to publish it? He put it away, saying something about how, at one time, short of money, he had sold the manuscript. To a friend, I presumed. Now he had it back. I am not sure whether he considered it his property or not. I am not sure what value he attached to this strange tale, what his attitude toward it was. Perhaps that it was not plausible. Or not printable. Or not readable.

He never mentioned it to me again.

To several of his fictions he wrote 'prefaces', and there exists one to *Le Mort*, representing an effort to situate it, to explain it biographically, to identify it. This preface was included in the 1966 issue which *L'Arc* devoted to his achievement, and I would like to reproduce it here in full.

Austryn Wainhouse

The original drafting of *Le Mort* dates back at least as far as 1944, to before June. In the spring of 1944 I was staying, alone, in Samois, a locality near Fontainebleau. Money — my civil servant's pay — was coming from Paris, I was then on sick leave, I had pulmonary tuberculosis, and once every fortnight I had to have a pneumothorax in Fontainebleau. It is three or four kilometers from Samois to Fontainebleau and up until just before the Americans arrived a bus service connected the two towns. I also had a bicycle, and my trips back and forth during the period when the American advance was forcing the Germans back finally had this outcome: shortly after Fontainebleau and Samois were liberated I went to have my lung collapsed: the doctor inserted the needle between my ribs again and again, his seven or eight tries were in vain. The air pocket was gone, entirely empty, it was dead. And that was how I found out I was cured: the disappearance of the air pocket, followed by a cessation of the microbe's activity, revealed that I was all right again; and since then I have not been bothered by any further tubercular trouble.

I returned to Paris during October. But before the Americans' arrival, not knowing for how long I might be cut off from funds in what could become difficult circumstances, I'd sold some manuscripts, among them the manuscript of *Le Mort*, to a Paris bookdealer.

So it is certain that I wrote *Le Mort* before Spring 1944. This text must have been done in 1943, but probably not earlier than that year. Where I wrote it I do not know: in Normandy (I was there in the latter part of 1942), in Paris in December of 1942 or in the course of the first three months of 1943? In Vézelay, between March and October of 1943? Or in Paris, between November 1943 and the spring of '44? Perhaps even in Samois, somewhere between April and June. Or again in Paris, at the Cour de Rohan, during the winter of '43–'44. I cannot remember. I am only sure of having recopied *Le Mort*, so as to have a few manuscripts to sell, before June 1944 (just as I am sure of having written this text after Spring 1942, which is when I fell ill; and I believe that the earliest date for it would be September–November 1942, the period when I was in Normandy).

There is in any case the narrowest tie between *Le Mort* and my stay in Normandy as the consumptive I then was; in Normandy not far from a village called Tilly (which in *Le Mort* I call Quilly). The Quilly inn is modeled upon the actual one in Tilly; the mistress of the inn in the book is the same as the Tilly innkeeper. I invented the other details except for the rain, which hardly stopped falling in October or November of 1942. Except also for the pitch black night when Julie knocks at the tavern door? Did I or did I not sleep at that inn? I don't remember, but it seems to me that I did. I further believe that in the taproom there were several farmhands wearing rubber boots, and even a player piano. Whatever, it was a sinister place, where anything could happen. In fine, I am sure that the atmosphere in the Tilly inn suggested the atmosphere for the inn in *Le Mort*. And lastly I am also sure, or almost, that I slept — alone — in that place, which terrified me.

The rest is related to the intense sexual excitement which dominated me throughout that mad November; in nearly complete solitude, I was then living not far from Tilly and about a kilometer away from where the girl who was my mistress lived. I was ill, in an obscure state combining physical fatigue, dread and exhilaration. It is hard to imagine what it was like, the mud, the rutted, bumpy little roads where

I cycled about in my shabby shoes. I then took most of my meals, but alone, in the houses of peasants.

I particularly remember one day hearing an airplane whose motor was in trouble. After those splutterings came a heavy thudding shock. I got on my bicycle. I at last found the spot where that German plane had come down. It was burning in a vast apple orchard: some nearby trees had been scorched and three or four bodies, flung around the wreck, lay dead in the grass. An English fighter had probably hit this enemy plane over the Seine Valley a short distance away, and it had got this far before crashing. A foot of one of the Germans was exposed, the sole of his boot had been ripped off. The dead men's heads looked shapeless. Flames must have got to them; there was nothing intact apart from that foot. It was the one human thing belonging to any of the bodies, and its nakedness, become claylike, was inhuman: the heat of the blaze had transfigured it; this object was not cooked, it was charred; snug inside the soleless uppers, it was diabolical, no, not that, but unreal, denuded, indecent in the extreme. I remained standing a long while that day, for that naked foot was looking at me.

In that Norman mud in '42 was I the philosopher worthy of the name I might perhaps have been? Today, when it is all I can do to think, dimly, that at some moment or other I was an authentic working philosopher, I no longer read anything. Philosophical activity (that which looks to me to be finished) in me loses its possible defense: in me what being a philosopher built collapses or, more precisely, has collapsed. I am certain only of having ruined in myself that which once made me a reader of Hegel, I who, without ever having taken anything but a fitful interest in Heidegger, even sometimes read Heidegger too (true, it was almost never in German). But what remains with me was at first a violent silence.

Will I be reproached if I have the weakness, finally, to confess that at present the kind of insignificance I am gradually turning into, which, I think, I have turned into, by

now even lacks the meaning my last phrase, 'a violent silence',
takes on? An instant ago, beside me, in a mirror, I caught sight
of an empty face: my face. It does not have the meaning of a
violent silence. Through the window what I am really
watching is 'the multitudinous smiling of the sea'.

Georges Bataille

When Edouard fell back dead an emptiness opened inside her, a prolonged shudder
went through her, and bore her upward like
an angel. Her bare breasts were rising in a
church seen in a dream where the feeling of
the irreparable was draining her. Standing
by the dead man, gone, transported, overcome in a slow ecstasy, smitten. She knew
herself to be desperate, but she was throwing
her despair to the winds. As he was dying
Edouard had beseeched her to take off her
clothes.

She had been unable to do it in time.
There she stood, disheveled: yanking at her
dress, only her bosom had popped into view.

MARIE REMAINS ALONE WITH
EDOUARD WHO HAS DIED

Time had just set at nothing the laws to which fear subjects us. She took off her dress and hung her coat over one arm. She was out of her mind and naked. She rushed out and ran in the night under the downpour. Her shoes clattered in the mud, the rain drenched her. She felt a need to move her bowels, held back against it. Come to a wood, she lay down amidst the soothing mildness of trees. She pissed against the earth, the urine wetting her legs. Upon the ground, quietly, in an absurd voice, crazily, she sang

'. . . my na-ked na-ked-ness
po-si-tive at-ro-cious-ness. . .'

Then she rose, put on her raincoat and ran through Quilly until she got to the door of the inn.

MARIE GOES OUT OF
THE HOUSE NAKED

Intimidated, she hesitated in front of the door, lacking the courage to enter. Shouts, the drunken singing of girls and men could be heard coming from within. She felt herself tremble, but from her trembling drew pleasure.

'I shall go in,' she thought, 'they shall see me naked.' She had to lean against the wall. She opened her coat and slid her long fingers into her crack. She listened, stiffened by excitement, upon her fingers she smelled the odor of unwashed sex. Inside the inn there was a loud uproar; even so, all was still. Rain fell, driven by tepid wind blowing through a cellar-like darkness. A girl sang, it was a working class song and sad. Heard outside in the night, the voice, low-pitched and muffled by the walls, was heart-rending. It ceased. Applause and the stamping of feet followed it, then cheers.

Marie sobbed in the dark. She wept in her helplessness, the back of her hand pressed against her teeth.

MARIE WAITS OUTSIDE
THE INN

Knowing she would enter, Marie trembled.

She opened the door, advanced three steps into the room: a draft blew the door shut at her back.

She recalled having dreamt of that door slamming forever shut behind her.

Farm-hands, the mistress of the inn and some girls were gazing at her.

She stood motionless in the entry; mud-spattered, hair dripping and ugliness in her glance. She appeared to have risen from the gusts of the night — the wind was to be heard outside. Her coat was covering her, but she opened it at the neck.

**MARIE ENTERS THE
TAPROOM OF THE INN**

In a low voice she asked if she could drink.

'A brandy?' asked the mistress from behind the bar.

She put a glass on the counter and filled it.

That was not what Marie wanted.

'A bottle and some big glasses,' she said.

Subdued as before, her voice was firm.

'I'll drink with them,' she added.

She paid.

A farm-hand in muddy boots addressed her shyly: 'Did you come to have some fun?'

'That's it,' said Marie.

She tried to smile: the smile sawed her face.

She stationed herself next to the boy, pressed her leg against his and taking his hand, placed it between her thighs.

'For Christ's sake,' moaned the boy when he touched the crack.

The others, flushed, kept still.

One of the girls came over, drew aside a skirt of the coat.

'Just look at that,' she said, 'nothing on!'

Marie let them go ahead and quickly downed a glass of alcohol.

'She really laps it up,' said the mistress.

A bitter belch was Marie's reply.

MARIE DRINKS WITH
THE FARM-HANDS

'That's it,' Marie said, sorrowfully.

Strands of wet black hair clung to her face. She shook her pretty head, straightened up, removed her coat.

A husky fellow who was drinking at the farther end of the room started toward her, lurching, his waving arms outflung. 'Snatch,' he brayed, 'this way with the snatch.'

'I'll snatch you,' the mistress darted at him. And she caught hold of his nose and tweaked it. He let out a yell.

'No,' said Marie, 'here's where you get a better hold.'

She went up to the drunk and unbuttoned his fly: the cock she brought to light slumped uncertainly.

The sight of it produced laughter all around.

Just like that, bold as you please Marie knocked off another glass.

Gently, eyes peering like searchlights, the mistress touched her behind at the divide:

'Makes your mouth water,' she said.

Marie filled her glass once again. The brandy went clucking down.

She swigged to kill. The glass fell from her hand. Her behind was colorless and deep-cleft. Its sweetness shed a glow throughout the room.

MARIE PULLS OUT A
DRUNKARD'S COCK

One of the peasants was standing off to one side, a look of hatefulness on his face. An overly handsome man, he was wearing high rubber boots, a little too new.

Marie came up to him, bottle in hand. She was tall and flushed. Her legs were shaky inside her loosening stockings. The young man took the bottle and swigged.

Then, in a loud voice, aggressively, he barked: 'All right, that's enough!' and banged the empty bottle down hard on the table.

Marie asked him whether he had something else in mind.

He smiled by way of answer: he seemed to feel he had it made with her.

He wound up the player piano. When he returned he lifted his arms and struck a pose, shuffled his feet; he looped a hand around Marie, they danced an obscene wiggle.

Marie threw herself into it body and soul, revolted, her head flung back.

MARIE DANCES
WITH PIERROT

Suddenly the mistress rose. 'Pierrot!' she cried.

Marie was falling: the handsome young man lost his hold upon her, stumbled.

The slender body which had slipped away landed on the floor with a dull thud.

'Whew,' said Pierrot, 'the bitch.'

He wiped his cuff across his mouth.

The mistress hurried over. She knelt and raised Marie's head carefully: saliva or rather drool spilled from her mouth.

A girl arrived with a moistened napkin.

Marie came to in a moment or so. She asked weakly for some brandy.

'Get a glass,' the mistress ordered one of the girls.

A glass was fetched. She drank. Then she asked for more.

The girl refilled the glass. Marie took it from her hands. She drank as if she were short of time.

Resting in the mistress' and one of the girl's arms, she raised her head.

'Another one,' she said.

MARIE FALLS
DEAD DRUNK

The farm-hands, the girls and mistress of the inn surrounding Marie waited for what she was about to say.

Marie murmured but one word:

'. . . dawn,' she said.

Then her head slumped heavily. She looked awful. Awful.

'What did she say?' the mistress asked.

Nobody knew what to answer.

MARIE WISHES TO SPEAK

Then the mistress spoke to the handsome Pierrot:

'Suck her.'

'How about if we put her on a chair?' one girl wondered.

Together several of them picked the body up and propped it in a sitting position upon the chair.

Pierrot, having got down on his knees, hoisted her legs so that they rested upon his shoulders.

The good-looking kid flashed a conquering smile and stuck his tongue in amidst the hairs.

Sick, illuminated, Marie seemed happy, she smiled without opening her eyes.

MARIE IS SUCKED BY PIERROT

She felt herself alight, chilled, but voiding it without stint sensed her life void itself into the gutter.

An unavailing desire kept her under strain: she would have liked to relieve herself. She imagined what a fright that would cause the others. She no longer felt sundered from Edouard.

Her cunt and her ass exposed: the smell of moist ass and moist cunt were setting her inwardly free and Pierrot's tongue, which was wetting her, gave her the impression of the chill of death.

Sotted on alcohol and tears and weeping not, she inhaled that chill, open-mouthed: drew the mistress' head to hers, unto decay opening the abyss of delight formed by her lips.

MARIE KISSES THE MISTRESS
UPON THE MOUTH

Marie thrust the mistress away and beheld that head, its hair askew, its features disordered by joy. Sweet drunkenness gave a radiance to the virago's face. She too was drunk, singing drunk: devout tears gathered in her eyes.

Regarding those tears and seeing nothing, Marie breathed bathing in the light of death.

'I am thirsty,' said she.

Pierrot was sucking away like a house afire.

The mistress hastily tendered her a bottle.

Marie swilled long draughts and drained it.

MARIE DRINKS FROM THE BOTTLE

. . . A scurry, a shriek of terror, a crashing of broken bottles, a froglike jerking of Marie's thighs. Commotion amongst the shouting youths. The mistress helped Marie to lie down upon the seat.

Her eyes remained vacant, enraptured.

Wind, squalls raged outside. Shutters were banging in the night.

'Listen,' said the mistress.

A howling of wind in the trees was heard, sustained and wailed like a mad-woman's call.

The door at that moment flew wide open, a blast blew into the room. The naked Marie was on her feet in a trice. She screamed: '*Edouard*!'

And the anguish in it made her voice one with the voice of the wind.

MARIE'S CRISIS

From out of that evil night a man emerged, struggling to close an umbrella: his rat-like silhouette stood out sharply in the doorway.

'Quick, my lord,' said the mistress, 'come in quick.' She swayed.

Without replying the dwarf-sized Count walked in.

'You are soaked to the skin,' the mistress went on, shutting the door.

There was a startling momentousness to the little man, broad and hunchbacked, his large head nested between his shoulders.

He greeted Marie solemnly, then turned to the farm-workers.

'Good evening, Pierrot,' said he, shaking hands with him, 'help me out of my coat if you will.'

Pierrot helped the Count rid himself of his coat. The Count pinched his leg.

Pierrot smiled. The Count distributed amiable handshakes.

'You will allow me?' he asked, making a bow. He seated himself at Marie's table, opposite her.

The Count called for some bottles.

'I've drunk so much,' said one girl, 'that I'm pissing on my chair.'

'Drink till you shit, dear child —'

And he broke off there, rubbing his hands.

Not without an air of detachment.

MARIE ENCOUNTERS A DWARF

Marie sat still looking at the Count and her head swam.

'Pour,' said she.

The Count filled the glasses.

Then she resumed, and in a very sober manner: 'I am going to die at dawn . . .'

The Count's steel-blue gaze scanned her.

His blonde eyebrows rose, deepening the wrinkles upon an excessively broad forehead.

Marie raised her glass and said, 'Drink up!'

The Count raised his glass too, and drank: together they downed their drinks at one swallow.

The mistress came and took a seat beside Marie.

'I am afraid,' Marie told her.

Her eyes remained fastened upon the Count.

Something like a hiccup shook her. In an uncontrolled voice she murmured in the older woman's ear: 'It's the ghost of Edouard.'

'What Edouard?' the mistress inquired in a whisper.

'He is dead,' Marie replied in the same whisper.

She caught the other's hand in hers and bit it.

'Bitch!' complained the bitten woman. But, pulling her hand free, she caressed Marie and as she kissed her shoulder, said to the Count:

'She's nice all the same.'

MARIE SEES THE
GHOST OF EDOUARD

Now it was the Count who asked, 'Who is Edouard?'

'You don't know who you are anymore,' said Marie.

With that her voice had broken. 'Make him drink,' she besought the mistress.

She appeared near to collapse.

The Count tossed off his glass but then he said: 'Alcohol doesn't do much for me.'

The solid little man with the over-sized head rested a bleak eye upon Marie, as if it were his intention to make her uncomfortable.

Whatever he looked at, it was in that same way, his head stiff between his shoulders.

'Pierrot!' he called.

The farm-hand drew near.

'This young thing,' said the dwarf, 'is getting a rise out of me. Would you care to sit down here?'

The youth once seated, the Count went on blithely:

'Be a good lad, Pierrot, take me in hand. I don't dare ask this child to do it . . .'

He smiled.

'Unlike you, she's not accustomed to monstrosities.'

At that point Marie climbed upon the seat.

MARIE CLIMBS UPON THE SEAT

'I'm scared,' said Marie. 'You look like a tombstone.'

He made no reply. Pierrot took hold of his member.

For impassiveness he did indeed resemble something of stone.

'Go away,' said Marie, 'or I'll piss on you if you don't . . .'

She climbed onto the table and squatted.

'You'll see me delighted if you do,' the monster rejoined. There was no play to his neck: only his chin moved when he spoke.

Marie pissed.

Vigorously Pierrot wanked the Count who received the urine full in the face.

The Count reddened and urine flowed over him. Pierrot's frigging was worth a fucking and the cock spat seed up the front of the waistcoat. In his throes the dwarf was racked by little shudders which made him jump from head to toe.

MARIE PISSES UPON THE COUNT

Marie kept on pissing.

On the table amidst the bottles and glasses she sopped herself with urine she caught in her hands.

She had it running down her legs, her ass and her face.

'Look,' she said, 'I'm a lovely sight.'

Crouched, her cunt level with the monster's head, she spread its lips horribly.

MARIE SPRINKLES HERSELF
WITH URINE

A venomous smile came over Marie's face.
A sinister, a nasty sight.
One of her feet slipped: they collided, her cunt against the Count's face.
He lost his balance and fell.
Both tumbled yelling to the floor amidst an incredible fracas.

MARIE TIPS OVER
UPON THE MONSTER

On the floor a dreadful wrestling ensued.

Marie went berserk, got her teeth into the Count's cock, the Count howled.

Pierrot hauled her away, pinned her at the wrists, her arms outflung; the others had hold of her legs.

'Let me go,' Marie wailed.

Then she was silent.

Finally it was all she could do to fight for her breath, her eyes shut.

She opened her eyes. Pierrot, red-faced, sweating, was on top of her.

'Fuck me,' she said.

MARIE BITES THE
DWARF'S COCK

'Stick her, Pierrot,' the mistress said.

They bustled around the victim.

Hemmed in by these preparations, Marie let her head subside. The others stretched her out flat, spread her legs apart. She was breathing rapidly, her breathing was noisy.

In its slow unfolding the scene recalled the slaughtering of a pig or the laying to rest of a god.

Pierrot once out of his trousers, the Count required that he remove everything else too.

The youth came on like a bull: the Count helped the pizzle enter. The victim thrashed and fought: a hand to hand combat, unbelievably bitter.

The others watched, dry-mouthed, astounded by this frenzy. The bodies linked by Pierrot's dick rolled upon the floor, struggling. At last, his back straining like a bow fully bent, the breathless boy let out a yell, foaming, Marie answering his shot with the spasm of one dying.

MARIE IS SCREWED
BY PIERROT

. . . Marie returned to her senses.

She heard birds singing in the boughs of a grove.

The songs, infinitely delicate, flitted with a swish from tree to tree. Lying in the wet grass she saw that the sky was clear: day was at that moment beginning to break.

She felt cold, gripped by an icy happiness, suspended in an unintelligible emptiness. Even though she sought, gently, to raise her head, and though she sank back from exhaustion upon the ground, she remained faithful to the light, to the foliage, to the birds thronging the wood. For a brief instant childhood timidities arose in her memory. She beheld, bending over her, the large and solid head of the Count.

MARIE LISTENS TO THE
BIRDS IN THE WILD WOOD

What Marie read in the eyes of the dwarf was the insistence of death: that face expressed only an infinite disenchantment, rendered cynical by a frightful obsession. Hatred surged up in her, and as death drew near she was very afraid.

She got up, gritting her teeth opposite the kneeling monster.

Upon her feet, she trembled.

She backed off, stared at the Count, and vomited.

'You see,' she said.

'Feel better?' the Count asked.

'No,' she replied.

She saw the vomit in front of her. Her torn coat covered her hardly at all.

'Where are we going?'

'To your house,' the Count told her.

MARIE VOMITS

'To my house,' groaned Marie. Again she felt dizzy.

'Are you the devil, wanting to go to my house?' she asked.

'Yes,' the dwarf replied, 'I've sometimes been told that I was the devil.'

'The devil,' said Marie, 'I shit in front of the devil!'

'You vomited a moment ago.'

'I'll shit now.'

She squatted and shat upon the vomit.

The monster was still upon his knees.

Marie leaned back against an oak-tree. She was sweating, her teeth chattered.

She said: 'All that, it doesn't amount to anything at all. But *in my house*, you're going to get a scare . . . you'll see . . . too late. . .'

She nodded her head, then strode fiercely over to the dwarf, seized him by the collar and shouted:

'Are you coming?'

'Willingly,' said the dwarf.

And he added, almost in a whisper:

'We're two of a kind.'

MARIE SHITS UPON THE VOMIT

Marie, who had heard what he said, gazed candidly at the Count.

He stood up. 'Never,' he murmured, 'does anyone speak to me in that manner.'

'You can go away, it's up to you,' she said. 'But if you come — '

The Count interrupted her sharply: 'I am coming with you. You are going to give yourself to me.'

Her mood was still angry. 'It's high time,' she said. 'Come on.'

MARIE LEADS THE COUNT HOME

They walked at a brisk pace.

The sun was coming up when they arrived. Marie pushed the gate. They went down a lane flanked by old trees whose crests were lit by golden sunshine.

Despite the vile mood she was in, Marie knew she was in agreement with the sun. She led the Count to her bedroom.

'It's all over,' she said to herself. She was at once weary, full of hatred, indifferent.

'Undress yourself,' she told him, 'I shall be waiting for you in the next room.'

The Count undressed himself unhurriedly.

The rays of sunlight coming through the leaves stippled the wall and the bright flecks were dancing.

MARIE AND THE DWARF
ENTER THE HOUSE

The Count was aroused.

His cock was long and ruddy.

His naked body and that cock had a devilish deformity. His face, bracketed between those angular and too high shoulders, was pale and mocking.

He desired Marie and confined his thoughts to this desire.

He came through the door. Wanly naked, she stood waiting for him beside the bed, tempting and ugly: drunkenness and fatigue had beaten her.

'What's wrong?' Marie asked.

The dead man, in disorder, was claiming all the space in the bedroom . . .

'I didn't know . . .' the Count stammered faintly.

He groped, clutched at a piece of furniture. His erection was failing.

Marie wore a ghastly grin.

'*It's over with*!' she said.

There was a stupid look about her as she showed a broken glass ampule in her right hand.

Then at last she fell.

MARIE DIES

*At last the Count caught sight of the two hearses,
proceeding slowly to the cemetery, one behind the
other.*

The dwarf hissed between his teeth:

'Foiled . . .'

He did not see the canal and slipped down into it.

*A heavy splash momentarily disturbed the silence
of the water.*

The sunshine remained.

MARIE FOLLOWS THE DEAD
MAN INTO THE GROUND

Ken Hollings

IN THE SLAUGHTERHOUSE OF LOVE

DARKNESS

I do not distinguish between freedom and
sexual freedom because depraved sexuality
is the only kind produced independently of
conscious idological determinations, the only
one that results from a free play of bodies and
images, impossible to justify rationally. . .
Because rational thought can conceive of
neither disorder nor freedom, and only
symbolic thought can, it is necessary to pass
from a general concept that intellectual
mechanisms empty of meaning to a single
irrational symbol.   *Ecrits posthumes,*
1922–1940
Lucidity excludes desire (or kills it, I don't
know): it dominates what remains.
                              L'Impossible
Night falls, certainly, but in the exacerbation of
desire.   *L'Expérience intérieure*

The death of Georges Bataille placed a language, already
corrupted by its own limits, in a state of duress from which it
can never free itself. The sexual act forces language onto the
threshold of direct experience — which is language's own
limit — and in so doing opens a dark sound in our
consciousness. The eroticism expressed in Bataille's writing
springs directly from this inescapable awareness. Beyond it
there is only the violent flux of our own sexual experience
through which corruption is revealed as our own sense of
coherence in the last throes of its being. Experience offers the
possibility of communication without coherence, something
which was termed in *Eroticism* as 'continuity': a condition in
which the individual is opened up and exposed in one
disruptive moment.

The sexual act poses a threat to our being because it places no limit on experience. During the act, the body no longer has limit or definition: it is dissolved into a storm of sensations which are violently superimposed and fluctuating. The effect that this has upon our consciousness can only be expressed negatively: in terms of exclusion and absence. The contemplation of the sexual act begins and ends in darkness and silence because it is contained by a law of exclusion which operates at the extreme limits of language and lucidity. In this darkness lies the beginning of a sexual knowledge which responds to the disruptive superimposition and confluence of desire and horror, affirmation and destruction. It is a response which lays waste and pollutes the purity of a historically dominant sexuality which, cleansed by social and cultural discourse, has been absorbed and rigidly defined by language.

Darkness, therefore, is neither static nor immutable: it is the fiercest expression of conflict. However, it does not resolve this conflict in expressing it, but affirms it. Since to resolve is finally to dominate and conserve meaning through exclusion, darkness is the denial of resolution. Seen in terms of social order, resolution establishes an account of experience in which the sexual act is rationalized out of existence. It is replaced by sexual transaction which comprises every practise — including social behaviour, language, representation — which renders sexual experience safe without banishing it completely. Whilst the act itself is performed in isolation, secrecy and silence, sexual transaction is socially pervasive. It helps regulate desire within a régime of production and consumption, giving it value by finally transforming it into work and exchange. Through this process it confers an identity upon us which the sexual act can only destroy.

This identity is constructed out of exchange and conservation, manifested in the deployment of commodities and energy, in which the act and transaction must inevitably oppose each other. This opposition also marks the origins of Bataille's philosophic inquiry into eroticism.

As language, consciousness and action can never establish a unity, sexual experience must by necessity be approached obliquely. In this respect Bataille utilized anthropology, literary criticism, history, economics and mysticism, all of which were radically transformed by their contact with the dark areas of sexual experience which had been forcibly placed outside discourse. This transformation exerts an influence which reaches far beyond Bataille's writings. History habitually blunts the effects of influence by incorporating them within the homogenizing processes inherent in our culture. Bataille's death, however, has not rendered his writings subject to this fate. Instead it endowed them with a profoundly disruptive power. The sexual act has been so closely circumscribed and defined by those processes implicit in social and cultural discourse that have rejected it, that its absence is clearly discernible. Eroticism is thus the extreme embodiment of an absence which Bataille's writings dramatized and expressed in terms of violence. As such, they constitute a break with the rationality of socially imposed identity. This is entirely appropriate to an age in which action has been refined into the purest dynamism of the gesture.

The gesture asserts itself through the rejection of language and logic. It found one of its most audacious and perceptive definitions at the beginning of this century when the Parisian journalist Laurent Tailhade said of a Black International bomb attack: 'What do a few human lives matter. *Si le geste est beau?*'

Bataille, in linking gesture to the violence of transgression and its discursive relationship with limit, reformulated them in terms of the social convulsions implicit in the art of sacrifice. Giving such precise form and meaning to violence affirms eroticism's status as ritual and makes it overflow all social boundaries. At a meeting of the secret society which he co-founded with Klossowski and Waldberg in the late thirties, Bataille called for 'an irrevocable ritual gesture — the enactment of a voluntary human sacrifice'.

Such a declaration has an optimistic, naive certainty to it which provokes both laughter and a darkly uneasy feeling. Although doomed to failure, it at least trivializes language's power. It is also symptomatic of a writer who never permitted his work to be reduced to the endless and hopelessly inadequate representation of sexual experience which is the fate of so much of our literature.

As a consequence Bataille's writing forbids interpretation by constantly obliging us to go beyond it. This leads us to a direct confrontation with the locked muscles, the cracking bones and the volatile communication expressed in the dark sacrifice of the sexual act itself.

NUDITY

But true nudity is bitter and maternal, silently white and fecal, like a cowshed; it is the nakedness of the baccanthe with pricks between her lips and legs; it is the ultimate terrestrial truth, both pithiatic and desiring to remain hidden. This truth like all Gods with their dying eyes open, always accepts condemnation.   *Le Petit*

Nudity is only death, and the most tender kisses have the after-taste of the rat.

L'Impossible

It was a question of confounding the human spirit and idealism with something *base*, to the extent that one recognised that the superior principles were irrelevant.   *L'Anus solaire*

Nudity is not a finite or absolute state: to be stripped naked is an experience which perpetually exceeds itself. The tearing away of clothing which exposes the flesh becomes a tearing away at the flesh itself. Naked, our being is laid open before the material reality of the body: but this body is no longer the idealized flesh handed down to us by a history of representation. The body is divested of the image of itself; an image which is static, unmarked and ideal and which confers value upon existence. In being stripped, the flesh ceases to be a sexual commodity; that is, a product of the social ordering of the physical presence in which identity remains intact and unviolated. The sexual commodity is the law of conservation, production and consumption made flesh. It is the imposition of history, and it converts our skin into a boundary which both contains and conceals us.

True nakedness is a confrontation with the charnal house of

the body: the knowledge of physical mortality and frailty. This knowledge exposes us to unrelenting risk and places us in a state of complete vulnerability which also exists prior to humiliation, torture or sacrifice: the experience of nakedness has been employed as a standard intimidation technique in prison cells throughout the world. Without the brutal horrors to be discovered within nudity, tenderness can be nothing but the pale and distant reflection of spiritual fear.

Being so close to death, the naked body will always be perceived as being on the point of embracing its own corruption. It is a permanent reminder of decay and generates a contagion in which lubricity reaches an unparalleled climax. Corruption is the stimulus of extreme licence and exposes our codes of sexual morality as the mere contours of desire and disgust. Putrefaction shows the body in disorder and sets itself against the rigid structures of socially regulated behaviour so violently that these structures will inevitably collapse. Bataille discovered the clearest manifestation of this socially destructive principle in the rituals of several oceanic cultures where a whole community would react to the death of their chief by entering into a prolonged period of frenzy. They gave themselves over to murder, looting, arson and sexual excess, continuing to do so until the decaying flesh had fallen away from the dead chief's bones. At this point normal patterns of behaviour reasserted themselves.

Social codes and discourse can accommodate the bare bones stripped of all flesh and can even endow them with a certain power. This implies that the breakdown of order and the degeneration into frenzy are not predominantly motivated by the experience of death, but by a specific perception of the body which is normally suppressed. Thus, putrefaction, in revealing the body to be unstable and base matter, deprives us of our sense of cohesive and inviolate identity. The artifice of propriety is torn apart: our flesh becomes dirt, and we actively embrace its foulness. In this excess the body's limit is transgressed, and it is exposed as a liquified flux of blood, urine, tears, sperm, sweat and excrement.

Nudity dramatizes to the point of destruction the duality of discontinuous being by throwing it into violent conflict with itself. In its purest state, true nudity is the birth of the perverse, a phenomenon which fragments and multiplies itself into any number of specific practices which arouse social condemnation. It is possible, however, to glimpse the perverse — unfixed and denying the imposition of meaning — refracted at points throughout our literature.

It is, for example, present in Baudelaire's 'Une Charogne'; a poem in which, over a series of carefully wrought stanzas, the image of a woman in the throes of sexual delirium is superimposed over a description of a cadaver rotting by the roadside in the summer heat. What begins as an intimate conversation with his lover becomes a passionate exultation in the inevitable corruption and decay of her body. Here the flesh becomes alive with larval insect life and graveyard vermin which both bite and kiss as they burrow into the corpse. A remarkable and unique text, produced by a man haunted by a traumatized morality: it is the expression of an erotic excess in which the body, fertile but doomed, is eternally laid bare.

PENETRATION

The act of violence that deprives the creature of its limited particularity and bestows on it the limitless infinite nature of sacred things is with its profound logic an intentional one. It is intentional like the act of the man who lays bare, desires and wants to penetrate his victims.   *L'Erotisme*

I imagine a nail of great length and her nudity. Her movements transported in fire make me reel physically, and the nail that I drive into her, I cannot leave there!   *L'Impossible*

Behind the curtains, the front room of the shop with its stone tiled floor was invitingly cool. Two freshly slaughtered lambs, hanging by their feet, were still slowly leaking blood; on the chopping block were some brains and large bones whose pearly white protuberances had an aggressive sort of nudity.

L'Abbé C

Erotic experience demands the total submission of the self to the immediate. By being forced into the present, physical sensation provokes a crisis of awareness in which consciousness inevitably exhausts and squanders itself. It is effectively displaced by the impossibility of grasping direct experience whilst being opened up to it. Eroticism is therefore a surrendering of the self to fear — but it is also an assertion of the will.

For an act to be decisive it must involve a certain amount of cruelty; that is, a complete disregard for the consequences. Guilt, remorse or pleasure — all that constitute the 'sense' of an experience — exist solely in the future. Since they can only confer meaning, the intensity of the moment renders them meaningless. The convulsions of the sexual act lay waste to everything but the deliberate commitment to an experience which violates the self. Fear and assertion exist together in that one moment beyond which there is nothing: no expectation, no object and no safety.

To reduce this experience to a series of physical components is to both limit and denature it. Whole symbol systems have been constructed out of the presence or absence of the phallus, the vagina, seminal fluid, blood and the anus. However the pursuit of a universalized order of meaning can only reduce and constrict in granting significance to human sexual anatomy through such systematic and interpretative configurations, they are deprived of much of their power. Erotic experience thus becomes congruent with the limits of the interpretative system imposed upon it. Most importantly the violence of the experience will be excluded from this relationship, since action is rendered subservient to the object and its place within the system. Violence, however, will not remain mute, although ordinary language cannot express it. Only in the dislocated logic, the limitless and enigmatic correspondences of metaphor can violence find its voice.

Metaphor dramatizes experience by not being subject to the reductive power of the intellect. By its very nature it cannot universalize.

Penetration, although central to procreation, is a mere fragment of erotic experience: it is not always present or even necessary. It can represent, however, a powerful metaphor for the decisive and irreversible commitment to act. Penetration is a stimulus to cruelty, it expresses the trauma of immediacy. As a metaphor, penetration is refracted and transformed throughout Bataille's texts and embodies an eroticism of laceration in which the body is opened up and the flesh violated. The piercing or the tearing out of the eye, the butcher's hacking away at meat to expose the bone beneath and the lover's desire to drive sharp nails into the loved one's

flesh all bring penetration close to murder. Casual, instinc-
tive, deliberate or compulsive, these actions all affirm the
possibilities which correspond to the crisis of fear and
assertion. All certainty is lost.

Action transgresses all limits through the excesses of the
violence it releases and, in so doing, places consciousness in a
condition of crisis. A dark fissure opens up in experience, and
the self is lost within it: the physical dynamics of penetration
are transformed into the liquefying and overflowing metaphor
of the wound. This marks consciousness indelibly with both
terror and intense pleasure and tears open all rational
responses to action. All the contradictions inherent in
commitment and the clash of sensations provoked by action
are expressed in the open wound which throws conflict into a
state of limitless play.

The perpetually open wound is the violence of direct
experience in its most tragic aspect. Its origins as a metaphor
are complex and date back to — and beyond — theosophic
conceptions of ecstasy and sacrifice. Out of it flow the fluids of
sexual excess through which the trembling of the body and the
closed, upturned eyes are experienced in the disruption of our
senses. Penetration, sacrifice and murder place no limit on
action: they are the fullest realization of thought and
sensation. Severed from their consequences, denying all
possibility of survival, decisive yet torn by conflict, they
indicate a point at which deliberate transgression gives way to
the condition of absolute freedom.

SACRIFICE

Hence love is based on a desire to live in anguish in the presence of an object of such high worth that the heart cannot bear to contemplate losing it. The fever of the senses is not a desire to die. Nor is love the desire to lose but the desire to live in fear of possible loss, with the beloved holding the lover on the very threshold of a swoon. At that price alone can we feel the violence of rapture before the beloved.

L'Erotisme

The sacrifice that we consume is distinguished from others in that he who executes the rite is affected by the sacrifice himself; he succumbs to it and loses himself along with his victim.

L'Expérience intérieure

Anguish is the fear of loss, the expression of the desire to possess. Recalcitrance in the face of communication stimulates desire as well as fear. Acknowledge the desire to possess and suddenly anguish turns to ecstasy.

L'Expérience intérieure

What finally frightens you and throws you into disorder is the knowledge that desire makes you its victim. In becoming an object of desire you become flesh, without identity and without meaning. In extreme forms of erotic experience, you become meat. Stripped of the identity imposed upon you by social and cultural discourse, there is nothing within which you can contain or preserve yourself. Possessed by desire, the individual is denied further recourse to exchange or transaction. Desire throws identity into turmoil: you cannot buy your way out.

The object of desire itself possesses the sense like a nervous disease. Desire inhabits — takes possession of — the body by subjugating it to the demands of intense need. The sexual act is a moment of total possession, rendered all the more extreme in its passion by the fear of loss. The possibility of ruinous loss throws the individual into disequilibrium because it destroys the precise balance of exchange and consumption which supports identity. Within any social order founded upon the conservation of objects, resources, energy and experience to be set against future transactions, deprivation becomes a source of real anguish.

True desire exists in the inescapable presence of unbearable loss. It invests the object with such high value that its absence becomes painful. The fear of this possible loss demands that the object of desire be experienced to the point of exhaustion. Debauchery is the affirmation of possession. It demands a total outlay of the self. This total outlay enters into a complex relationship with loss which carries over into the general economic ordering of behaviour. However, both are essentially anti-social in nature as their existence is explicitly hostile to the principles of conservation.

This hostility can be formulated in terms of sacrifice; an act of conscious and ruthless devastation with no other aim than its own completion. The sacrifice of objects, animals and humans endows them with a higher worth than that imposed by normal patterns of production and consumption. Impending destruction elevates them above mere exchange. This evanescent quality exhausts the order of values inherent in the society in which the sacrifice takes place. The shattering of objects, the spilling of blood and the tearing open of the flesh provoke a delirium which is not denatured for having been considered in terms of outlay and conservation. Sacrifice bestows a value beyond value: the point at which desire and its object meet. It provides a violent correlative to the sexual act. In this respect it indicates a movement from the purely instinctual to the deliberate which is dependent upon excessive indulgence rather than self-denial: it will as a consequence infect an entire community.

The transitions involved, however, are not possible outside an economic system. Bataille traces a history of eroticism which parallels, and is dependent upon, a history of economic activity and its relation to work. It details the separation of eroticism and work from the reproductive urges of animal sex. This separation is conditioned by the awareness and fear of death as loss and absence to which the responses of eroticism and work are markedly divergent. Where work conserves and regulates human energy, eroticism squanders and exhausts it: they exclude and interpenetrate each other in a play of limit and transgression.

Like sacrifice, work and eroticism are highly organized forms of activity which require preparations through which desire is granted a presence within the cultural life of a society. In this respect Bataille is correct in describing eroticism from a shifting series of historical perspectives. As a cultural product, eroticism has no fixed or established conventions: as a social phenomenon based on fluctuations of desire and horror, it perpetually changes. However, in being linked to work and a system of production and consumption, eroticism's historical presence is severely conditioned by them. Production and consumption structure history in terms of progress and it is hard not to consider a history of eroticism from the vantage point of some idea of advancement. To speak today of sacrifice as it relates to the sexual act is to invert such a conception. It exposes an industrial society's nostalgia for some form of pre-capitalist culture based on a utopian intra-uterine life of desire and emphasizes its falsity. It negates any dream that remains of a fall from sexual grace which can somehow be reversed by a social and cultural progression towards the eradication of licence. Instead sacrifice reveals the origins of a harsh and delirious excess.

VIOLENCE

Only literature could escape the game of the transgression of the law, without which the law would have no meaning independent of an order to be created. Literature cannot assume the task of ordering collective necessity. . . Literature, in fact, like transgression of the moral order, is dangerous.

Literature and Evil

But silence cannot do away with the things that language cannot state. Violence is as stubbornly there just as much as death, and if language cheats to conceal universal annihilation, the placid work of time, language alone suffers, language is the poorer, not time and violence.   *L'Erotisme*

If one were to ascribe me a place within the history of thought, it would be, I believe, for having discerned the effects, within our lives, of the moments at which discursive reality disappears, and for having drawn from the description of these effects a disappearing light: this light may be blinding, but it also announces the opacity of the night; it announces only the night. *Oeuvres complêtes*

Violence exists in the moment when the eye turns upwards into the head, when inversion is complete and total. The darkness of the upturned eye is not the absence of light but the process of seeing taken to its limit. It is therefore impossible to speak of a conflict between darkness and light but rather a thorough derangement of the senses. The violence of this experience constitutes the end of the eternal separation of the ideal from the base and the pure from the polluted. They are no longer in opposition to each other; their relationship is inverted. Inversion transcends opposition; conflict is not resolved but placed in a state of play within which no limit is imposed upon desire: all that violates the sensibilities becomes an intense delight. To desire that which is base, depraved or degrading is an act of revolt without aim or reason.

Beyond sense and logic and the divisions they foster within our experience there is the severe disequilibrium of the senses which disrupts and holds sway over consciousness. In Bataille's fiction this imbalance takes full possession of the characters, consuming them both physically and emotionally. Anguish, desire and fear provoke a delirium in which bodies shake and convulse, becoming prey to fever and sensations of extreme cold. Simultaneously awareness is heightened and intensified to almost painful levels of clarity. Stark correspondences are established between this turbulence and the malevolent skies under which the figures in Bataille's fiction move. At times there is only a vast dome of unending darkness which is terrifying in its unchanging monotony, at others it becomes one of a glaring, almost unbearable light which infuses the scenes being acted out beneath it. Most often it is a sky violently agitated by a howling storm: at night the lightning flashes in the darkness. This flash, as it is described by the un-named narrator of 'Histoire des rats', the first section of *L'Impossible*, is an instantaneous moment of inversion. The lightning and the night sky illuminate and obscure each other simultaneously. The moment is gratuitous and random, following the dictates of its own reason. Like the gesture, it rejects common language and conventional logic, not by negating them but by giving free play to the conflicts which they engender. Through inversion, experience is rendered both limitless and tragic at that moment when subject and object have vanished; when it is no longer possible to see who is speaking. In the intensity of sexual experience inversion occurs when the voice becomes an exhalation of breath, a transition which releases the full power to communicate. It is communication made total.

An approach to this transition through language, however oblique, creates a vocabulary of elision, superimposition and unqualified contradiction. They indicate a totality of experience even if ultimately they cannot replace it or articulate it fully. Bataille employs a large number of terms and expressions without limiting their meaning through precise definition: they become viscous, and their power to communicate stems from their perpetual flow, and regrouping. This is most apparent in his theoretical writings which offer a virtually unlimited series of points of departure rather than a cohesive linear argument. Similarly, a whole study could be made of the use of simile in Bataille's fiction where normally unrelated images strain and buckle under the pressure of being linked together in unstable union. By overturning systems of meaning in which an exclusive definition is guaranteed, Bataille releases the violence of thought. No longer abstracted or contained, thought embraces sensation and becomes debased and polluted. Darkness and light are suddenly and instanteously reversed.

Perhaps there is nothing beyond this violence except the will to endure and survive it, however much it may alter or disrupt. Language exists permanently on the edge of a state of collapse beyond which there is the eternal possibility of an experience freed from division and the constraints of a system of relative values and meanings. Order fragments consciousness, but the annihilation of order is not enough and never will be enough: that is merely a return to some mythical state of grace, a cellular, animal awareness. The inversion of order excites not only violence — that is, the derangement of the senses — but also the consciousness of that violence. The play of transgression and limit in this respect is crucial. The limit which is broken without a thought means nothing and nullifies transgression. There is no ideal, no code, no ultimate aim except revolt for its own sake: that is an assertion of the self which is at once dark, violent and irrevocable.

Georges Bataille

AUTOBIOGRAPHICAL NOTE

Born, Billom (Puy-de-Dôme), September 10, 1897. Family of peasant stock for two or three generations, originally from the Ariège, Puy-de-Dôme, and the Cantal. Father blind (prior to [G.B.'s] birth) and paralyzed (1900).

Schooling at Reims lycée, very bad student, almost expelled in January 1913, refuses to continue schooling and stays idle at home until October, but agrees to enter Epernay secondary school as a boarder. Now becomes a good student. Brought up with no religious instruction, now leans toward Catholicism, and is formally converted in August 1914.

Having fled to safety with his mother's family in the Cantal, is called up for service in January 1916. Falls gravely ill, is discharged in 1917. Briefly considers becoming a priest, or rather a monk. Enters the School of Paleography and Library Science in November 1918, is regularly at the top of his class, but graduates second.

Two months in England in 1920. Following a stay with the Benedictines of Quarr Abbey on the Isle of Wight, suddenly loses his faith because his Catholicism has caused a woman he has loved to shed tears.

Upon graduation from the School of Paleography is named fellow of the School of Advanced Hispanic Studies in Madrid (later the Casa Velásquez). Enthusiasm for bullfights; witnesses death of Granero, one of Spain's most popular matadors (certainly the most popular after Belmonte) in the Madrid arena.

Enters the Bibliothèque nationale as a librarian in July 1922.

Is convinced, from 1914 on, that his concern in this world is with writing and, in particular, with the formulation of a paradoxical philosophy. Reading of Nietzsche in 1923 is decisive. Resolving to travel, begins study of Russian, Chinese, and even of Tibetan, which he quickly abandons. Translates, with collaborator, book by Leon Chestov from the Russian (1924).

Forms friendship with Michel Leiris, then with André Masson, Théodore Fraenkel. Enters into contact with the surrealists, but the result is mutual hostility between himself and André Breton. In 1926, writes a short book entitled *W.-C.* (this book, of violent opposition to any form of dignity, will not be published and is finally destroyed by its author), then, in 1927, *The Solar Anus* (published, with Masson's etchings, by the Galerie Simon in 1931). The virulently obsessive character of his writing troubles one of his friends, Dr Dausse, who has him undergo psychoanalysis with Dr Borel. The psychoanalysis has a decisive result; by August 1927 it put an end to the series of dreary mishaps and failures in which he had been floundering, but not to the state of intellectual intensity, which still persists.

Marriage in 1928. Meeting at that time with Georges Henri Rivière through the publication, in 1929, of *Documents*, an art magazine containing a miscellaneous section edited by Bataille under the somewhat remote supervision of Carl Einstein. Bataille publishes a certain number of articles in this journal, his earliest published writings, of which the first is a text on Gallic coins admired by him. (Breton will, following a misunderstanding, come to see this article as an attack on Gallic art.) The mutual hostility of Bataille and Breton at that time brings Bataille into closer relation with ex-members of the surrealist group; in addition to friends such as Leiris and Masson, Jacques Baron, Jacques-André Boiffard, Robert Desnos, Georges Limbour, Max Morise, Jacques Prévert, Raymond Queneau, Georges Ribemont-Dessaignes, Roger Vitrac. These are largely the names listed at the end of the

Second Surrealist Manifesto (published in *La révolution surréaliste*, 1929), in which they are subjected to a violent attack, ending with the denunciation of Georges Bataille, considered to be planning the formation of an antisurrealist group. This group never existed; nevertheless those singled out by the Second Manifesto were agreed upon the publication of *Un cadavre* (a title already used by the future surrealists on the death of Anatole France), a blistering indictment of Breton (which in no way prevented most of them, including Bataille himself, from later reconciliation).

Documents, the journal which had been at the origin of these polemics owing to its publication of numerous articles by the authors of *Un cadavre*, ceased to exist in 1931. Shortly afterward, Bataille entered the Democratic Communist Circle, which published *La critique sociale* (from 1931 to 1934) under the editorship of Boris Souvarine. Bataille published several long studies, including 'The Notion of Expenditure', 'The Psychological Structure of Fascism', and, in collaboration with Raymond Queneau, 'Critique of the Foundations of the Hegelian Dialectic'. Bataille was then a close friend of Queneau, who worked daily at the Bibliothèque nationale, gathering documentation for a book on 'literary madmen' (which, some years later, ended in the publication of *Enfants du Limon*).

The Democratic Communist Circle ceased to exist in 1934. At that time Bataille, after several months of illness, underwent a serious psychological crisis. He separated from his wife. He then wrote *Blue of Noon*, which is in no way the narrative of this crisis, but which can be considered as reflecting it.

Bataille personally took the initiative in 1935 to found a small political group which, under the name of Counter-attack, united some former members of the Communist Circle and, following a definite reconciliation with André Breton, the whole of the surrealist group. Some meetings of Counterattack took place in the 'Grenier des Augustins' (now Picasso's studio), with the last, on January 21, 1936, dedicated to the death of Louis XVI. Breton, Maurice Heine, and Bataille took the floor.

Counterattack was dissolved at the end of the winter. (The supposed pro-fascist tendency on the part of certain of Bataille's friends, and, to a lesser degree, of Bataille himself. For an understanding of the element of truth in this paradoxical fascist tendency, despite its radically contrary intention, one should read Elio Vittorini's *The Red Carnation*, together with its strange postscript. There is no doubt that the bourgeois world as it exists constitutes a provocation to violence and that, in that world, the exterior forms of violence hold a fascination. Be that as it may, Bataille considers, at least since Counterattack, that this fascination can lead to the worst.)

With Counterattack dissolved, Bataille immediately resolved to form, together with those of his friends who were former members (these included Georges Ambrosino, Pierre Klossowski, Patrick Waldberg), a 'secret society' which, turning its back on politics, would pursue goals that would be solely religious (but anti-Christian, essentially Nietzschean). This society was formed. Its intentions are in part expressed in the journal *Acéphale*, published in four issues between 1936 and 1939. The *Collège de sociologie*, founded in March 1936, represented, as it were, the outside activity of this 'secret society'; this 'college', whose domain was not all of sociology, but rather the 'sacred,' expressed itself publicly through a series of lectures. The founding members were, in addition to Bataille, Roger Caillois and Michel Leiris. Lewitsky, Jean Paulhan, and Georges Duthuit lectured there.

It is difficult to talk of the 'secret society' properly so-called, but certain of its members have apparently retained the impression of a 'voyage out of the world'. Temporary, surely, obviously unendurable; in September 1939, all of its members withdrew. Disagreement arose between Bataille and the membership, more deeply absorbed than Bataille by immediate concern with the war. Bataille, in fact, had begun in 1938 to practice yoga, but really without close adherence to the precepts of the traditional discipline, in considerable chaos and in a state of mental turmoil pushed to the extreme. A death occurring in 1938 had torn him apart. It was in complete solitude that he began, in the opening days of the war, to write *Le coupable*, in which he describes a mystical experience of a heterodoxical nature in the course of development and, at the same time, some of his reactions to the events then taking place. At the end of 1940 he meets Maurice Blanchot, with whom links of admiration and agreement are immediately formed. Toward the end of 1941, before *Le coupable* has been completed, Bataille begins to write *L'expérience intérieure*, completed before the end of the following year.

Owing to an infected lung, he is forced to leave the Bibliothèque nationale in April 1942. In 1943 he settles in Vézelay; there he remains until 1949. (*On Nietzsche, Memorandum.*) While living in Vézelay he founds a monthly review, *Critique*, in 1946. By dint of frequent trips to Paris he succeeds, in collaboration with Eric Weil and then with Jean Piel, in endowing this publication, in which he publishes many studies, with a definite authority.

If thought and its expression have become his main area of activity, this has not been without repeated attempts, within the limits of his means, at experiences lacking apparent coherence, but whose very incoherence signifies an effort to comprehend the totality of possibility, or to put it more precisely, to reject, untiringly, any possibility exclusive of others. Bataille's inspiration is that of a sovereign existence, free of all limitations of interest. He is, indeed, concerned with *being*, and being as *sovereignty*, with transcending the development of means. At issue is the attainment of an end over and above means — at the price, if necessary, of an impious disturbance. Philosophy, for example, for Bataille comes down to acrobatics — in the worst sense of the word. The issue is not that of attainment of a goal, but rather of escape from those traps which goals represent.

We must not elude the task incumbent upon all men, but reserve a share of sovereignty, a share that is irreducible. On this level it is an attitude which follows in the wake of religious experience, but the religious experience freed from the quest for means, that religious experience which must be an end if it is anything at all. There is work on Bataille's part, but it is an effort to escape, an effort of release toward a freedom that is direct.

Georges Bataille
Translated by Annette Michelsen
(October Magazine 36)